**frustrated
young
men**

Frustrated Young Men

A Collection of Short Fiction

John O'Brien

PulpLit Publishing

PulpLit Publishing
762 South St.
Needham, MA
www.PulpLit.com

*Back Cover Photo © Ray Hatfield
Front Photo © John O'Brien
Cover Design by John O'Brien*

First American Edition 2003

ISBN 0-9746196-0-4

Acknowledgements

I'd like to thank my family, and of course Rebecca, who was the best copy editor a guy could have. She has put up with many early morning writing bouts, and much else.

These pieces are the end result of innumerable fiction writing workshops and writing instructors, to whom I am eternally grateful.

For Mary T. O'Brien

Introduction: An Interview with the Author

Interviewer: First I'd like to thank you for sitting down with me today.

Author: Oh, believe me. It is my pleasure. Anything to get the word out – I'm very excited.

I: You and some of the characters in your collection of short fiction seem to have a lot in common. You're a young man; are you also frustrated?

A: [*Laughing almost girlishly*] Well, I mean, you can't help but draw from your own experiences. So, yes, these characters are a lot like me. And I guess you could say that I am frustrated, yes.

I: By what?

A: By life, and the publishing scene. I feel like writing [fiction] is one of those endeavors where a work should be measured solely on its own merits. But that doesn't seem to happen; often it's who you know, or what you've published before, or how good a story it would make to publish you. People love to be part of the rags-to-riches-I-overcame-something story, and when they buy the book of an author who is cast in that light, they can be part of it, because their money is what is *creating* that story.

It becomes part of that whole postmodern thing, where people look to the books they buy or the sofa they own to define them. I mean, I decided to go with PL [PulpLit Publishing] because I felt like they understood me, both as a writer and as a person. Also, when I weighed my other options, I realized that nobody wanted to publish a collection of short stories from a previously unpublished author. Usually I would have to have been published in some banner publications, like *The Atlantic* and *The New Yorker*, to get my own collection. That seemed unlikely.

Also, due to policies against simultaneous submissions, getting each of my short stories published somewhere big could have taken *days*, maybe even *weeks.* With PL the whole turnaround time was very short.

Finally, due to the unconventional nature of my stories, I felt like traditional publishers may not have been interested.

I: What do you mean by "unconventional"?

A: Let me tell you a Chinese parable by way of example. It's very often associated with Zen Buddhism, and I think it may be relevant here.

It starts with this traveler who is walking along and is set upon by a tiger. He runs, and the tiger chases him, until he comes to the edge of a cliff. With the tiger hot on his heels, he catches hold of a thick vine and swings himself over the edge.

Above him the tiger snarls. Below him he hears another snarl, and looks down, and down below, wouldn't you know it, but there is another tiger, peering up at him. He's hanging halfway down a cliff suspended between two tigers. Just when he thinks things can't get any worse, two mice— a white mouse and a black mouse— begin to gnaw at the vine. He can see that they are quickly eating through it.

He notices a wild strawberry plant growing from the canyon face with a single perfect ripe red strawberry. He takes the strawberry into his mouth and savors its succulent flavor, and in that moment what could taste sweeter?

I: And?

A: That's the whole story.

I: I don't get it.

A: That's what I'm trying to illustrate. A certain Eastern way of thinking creates certain plots and stories that may not come to what we here in the West feel is a very satisfying conclusion. But there is still a point.

I: If you had to pick a favorite among the stories in this collection, which one would you pick?

A: *Toby Grey*, probably.

I: Why that one? I have to say, I was a little, er –

A: Offended?

I: Not offended so much as surprised. There seems to be a lot of sex and drugs, without much point.

A: That was partly my point. Here is a teenager, sixteen, seventeen, who is taking drugs, having sex, and is all emotionally torn up about it. I think most publishers wouldn't touch that story with a ten-foot pole; not because of the subject matter in particular. People love stories about incense and drugs and abuse of any kind. I think they'd turn it down because his angst is in essence sourceless. But I felt that it was important to accurately depict what being a teenager was like. We all know that some kids have sex early on, that they try drugs, but the only time it seems we're allowed to talk about it is when we're berating it.

3

Introduction

I: Do you feel that the main character in *Toby Grey* is a lot like you?

A: Oh, no. Well, a little. Maybe just a little.

I feel like teen angst stories are given a bad reputation. Some of this is deserved. Mostly I think it is because most teen angst stories are written by teenagers, which means the stories lack any psychic distance between the experience and the analysis of the experience. The problem isn't so much the classic story of love and loss and emerging from innocence, which so many teen stories are about; the problem is this lack of perspective.

So with *Toby Grey*, I was trying to create a teenager that had perspective, was aware of his problems, but couldn't do anything to address them.

I think too often people seem to belittle an experience because it is cliché, which does a great disservice to most of humanity. I mean, let's face it, most people's lives aren't all that unique when looked at from a really broad perspective. But does that mean that their experience isn't genuine or valid? I don't think so.

I also wanted to talk about what a person may be giving up when they go on antidepressants. I knew all these kids who were on Prozac and lithium growing up. And you have to wonder why. Was it to make them happy, or because people were a little uncomfortable with them, you know? Stuff like that.

Also, I wanted to examine how it always seemed to me the most entertaining and interesting people were the ones who were fucked up – can I say "fuck"?

I: Yes, it's okay.

A: I always felt like the people who were screwed up were the ones who were the funniest. And so I have to ask, what are they giving up when they go on SSRIs [Selective Serotonin Reuptake Inhibitors]?

I: What advice would you give any other young writers who are similarly frustrated and desperately want to be published?

A: Contact PulpLit Publishing [*again, that strange, almost girlish laugh*]. But seriously, I think young writers just like me have to ask themselves what they're really looking to accomplish. If you're just looking to get published, that's relatively easy. Speaking very literally, anybody with a good ink-jet printer can get published.

I think most people don't write for money, or fame, or even art. They write because they have something to say, and they want someone to listen. They want to get published, I think, because they want approval, and to be let into the "in crowd" I was talking about.

If they can, they should look into those POD [print-on-demand] publishers, though probably not ExLibris; they look like they rip people off. That's what I hear. But other printers, like Ion Systems. Because after they've gotten it out there, they can really think about why they're writing in the first place. I mean, if it's to share their thoughts and feelings, why not just start a blog somewhere on the Internet? So I think that is something to think about.

I: Why do you write?

A: I write because I feel a need to try to communicate with other people. Probably selfish reasons— I want to be heard.

To be paid attention to. So, like most people who want attention, I just make up stories that I hope other people will find entertaining.

I: What are you working on next?

A: I've been thinking about maybe doing a novel written from three or four points of view at once. So each moment of the story would have three or four lines simultaneously depicting the action, like this:

I reach for the salt. Why can't Ralph sit up straight?
Da is reaching for the salt over me; why doesn't he ask?
Da is reaching. Ralph is slouching; I bet he's going to get it.

I: That sounds interesting.

A: I think so.

The Writer

Every morning for about an hour he would write in a simple spiral-bound notebook by his bedside, his thin scrawl stretched wide across the page, recording rapid-fire his morning ideas and what he could remember of his dreams.

He kept a stylish flat up in midtown New York, his bed and duvet always ruffled and unmade. A junior analyst at Goldman Sachs still pulls in enough to live well, if cramped.

His studio apartment had enough space for his desk and massive bed, a setup suitable for eating pizza and watching a movie, perhaps with the occasional guest.

And every evening, after starched shirt and pressed tie were removed, he would settle down again for an hour or two and type type type on his little laptop.

He was working on a novel, he'd tell himself. But mostly he would write in his diary about how much he wanted to write, how much he wanted to be a writer.

Sometimes he could feel his mind burning, ripe with ideas, each thought rolling around like slick mercury eating through the top of his skull. He would ride the train home from work and feel each precious thought smoking, like raw egg fallen on a gas burner. As he closed the door to his apartment and hung his jacket, they would already be half gone, like the afterimage of a sunset against his closed eye-lids, floating and translucent, and lost when he sat down late every night, after a long day of nothing, to type and write and rhapsodize about his own stupidity.

It was hard sometimes, keeping on with the day to day with red-hot iron slicing through his brain. Writing by hand every morning and typing every evening; it was almost too much for a stock analyst to handle. Ah, well. They say Einstein was a patent clerk when he was twenty-five.

Over diary and scone one morning he found that he was once again stuck. He stared at the open window, pondering his view of the brick wall of the building across the way, and wondered why the muses who deemed others worthy hadn't blessed him.

Maybe it was his current focus at work, precious metals, though precious metals had been hot as of late, with gold topping two hundred dollars an ounce. Maybe he needed to write longer in the morning.

It was over drinks with a successful banker friend later that day that he was handed his epiphany.

"San Francisco," his friend said, chomping on the olives from his martini.

"I dated this chick once, she was from San Francisco. Real oat bran type. She used to paint the walls. Great in bed. She was from San Francisco. Everybody is a fucking artist. Something in the water I think, or maybe it's the weather."

His banker friend pointed his little drink sword at Alex accusingly.

"You should move there and give it a go."

So that's what he did.

Our hero's first impressions as recorded in his diary the next morning: "A small city. Airport is quaint and dates from the '70s. Flying into SFO was like landing in an industrialized suburb. Factory town. Feels more like McClary in Iowa than a real city. Apartment I chose blind through a broker is larger than comparably priced space in NY, but not by much. Worse parking than NY. Research why there are so many steep hills."

He introduced himself in the Goldman satellite office and spent the first couple of weeks getting up to speed on his new specialty, consumer durables. A transfer was easy for such a bright young man full of promise. He was welcomed heartily, then ignored.

Alex started a new routine. After rousing himself at five, he would type two hours in the morning and get drinks in the evening with coworkers. He started wearing tight-cut jackets, putting money in the bank.

Ideas would come while he was on the Muni heading downtown from Russian Hill. He would jot them into a little pad he kept in his back pocket, which seemed quite a common thing to do. His friend was right; even the homeless people seemed to be writers, each with their own spiral-bound notebook. He wondered whether they all felt the pressure to produce, whether maybe they all brought it on each other.

After a couple of weeks of getting up at five, he realized he couldn't keep burning the candle at both ends, and quit. Two hours a day makes ten hours per week of writing; even so, he had only the beginning of a novel about a white detective in Harlem to show for it. He'd only gotten ten pages into the novel when the detective got beaten to death, and after that he'd been stuck.

When he quit, his supervisor, Mr. Stevens, laid his hand on his shoulder and told him he was sorry to see him go and to pack up his desk by the end of the day.

He got a job with flexible hours, at the Quiet Desperation Bookstore and Café on Haight Street, which gave him more time to write. He felt that he'd really start to get into it now, he'd really get a grip on where he was going, what he wanted to be, etc.

Of course, he couldn't afford to live in the place on Russian Hill anymore, so he moved out to the Sunset and in with an Asian girl, Jane Phen, a smoker who liked cats.

"I only care that you pay rent," she told him, and left him alone. She was gone five days out of the week and on Sundays meditated in the living room to a tape of waves and rain, called *Sounds of Water*.

He settled into a new writing routine, four hours of typing every other day, and began to feel like he was making some real progress.

One of his fellow workers at Quiet Desperation was a young woman named Alyssa MacIntyre. She was eighteen, taking a break before the big leap to college. Or rather, she has declined to make that decision as of yet. They both worked the same seven-hour floor shifts, Monday, Wednesday, and Friday from 10 to 5, with two five-minute breaks and a half hour for lunch.

The MacIntyre clan wasn't exactly overjoyed with young Alyssa's decision, but the deadlines had passed before they realized she had not sent out even a common application, and they were unable to do anything, at least not until winter. For the summer and fall, Alyssa was doing just fine working at the Q.D.

Alex had thought that he would write during the day at work, but the tourist crowd broke the quiet solitude he'd expected. Sporadic journal writing at work subsided eventually, and he contented himself with writing at his new desk on Tuesday and Thursday, and getting up rather late, at eight, and watching the fog burn off Golden Gate Park.

He got to noticing that Alyssa kept a notebook herself through much of the day, an intricate leather assemblage that she would occasionally take out to jot down a note, then rewrap and stuff into the voluminous pockets of her sweatshirt.

Alex found her sweatshirt fascinating. It seemed part of a uniform for Alyssa. He wore the same starched shirts he used to wear at Goldman out of habit— now sans tie— though there wasn't a formal dress code at the Q.D. He felt propriety had to be kept, whatever the circumstances.

Alyssa felt no such restraints. Her hooded sweatshirt was large enough to hide purloined books, drugs, or a thin knife, and her baggy pants rolled off her in trailing ruffles that dragged behind her worn sneakers. She had gentle freckles speckled about her cheeks, and, he imagined, maybe along her arms and broad shoulders and back, and she had green eyes.

She would shuffle into work ten or fifteen minutes late every morning, with a mocha latte and a low-slung home-made backpack of colored patches dangling over one shoulder.

He found her strange and unnerving. She had a quiet assurance he felt must be born of ignorance and naïveté, and she did not show him the least concern. Her red hair was tied in a complex bundle of knots and string, a wild braid that he found vaguely repulsive. She smelled of musty hay and tawny sweat, or at least that is how he described her in his diary. He found her unfathomable and was petrified of her.

After four weeks of working together, he asked her out for coffee.

She could write brilliantly.

Sometimes, in the mornings before she awoke, he would stretch out naked and extract her journal from her bag. After undoing the ties, he would run his fingers along the purple and blue stones embedded in the cover, and turn the gold-leaf pages until he came to her most recent entry. Sometimes she would draw pictures, these thick pen sketches (how could she sketch in pen, he wondered, with so little room for error). They were amateur works, with occasional commentary, though somewhere in them lurked the same broad gentle spirit he sensed in her writing.

Sometimes her journal entries were wisps of everyday happenings; sometimes they were half-finished thoughts he felt she could have turned into full-fledged stories.

"The boy dragged his shirt behind him, the fabric wet and smearing the pavement with the smell of urine," she would write, and he wasn't sure whether it was the beginning of a novel or a record of something she had actually seen somewhere in the city.

She rarely seemed to write about him. He liked to turn to a sketch she'd made of him, one that made him look much more pensive and roguish than he felt. She titled it "Slow

Day," and it depicted him leaning over a counter at the Q.D., reading a book.

She would wake up slowly in the morning, her red mop of hair disheveled and quickly bound up, her only breakfast strong coffee. She rarely slept over. Dating did not affect their relationship at work at all. If her parents gave her a hard time about it, she never told him. Jane Phen raised her eyebrows when she first saw them, but said nothing.

Alex bought a new notebook covered in smooth calfskin and redoubled his efforts to write.

After a couple of weeks of sporadically sleeping at his place, Alyssa started appearing in his dreams. Most often she was a loose-limbed goddess with glassy eyes. He envisioned her as a giant, her broad smooth limbs stretching out high above him, much as a flea must imagine its host.

One night when Jane was out, after they'd made themselves miso soup and nigiri, he showed Alyssa the beginning of his novel about the detective in Harlem. She sipped red wine and flipped through the pages while he started the dishes.

After she was done she said it was very good, and they split a joint and made love.

It was later that night, while they were both drifting off to sleep, that she asked him if he had ever heard the story about the boy and the harp.

"No. Is it Middle Eastern?"

He could feel her turn on her side, her fingertips resting softly against his bare back.

"No. I think it's Dutch."

"No, I haven't."

"Let me tell it to you. Once upon a time, in a land far away, there was a carpenter and his wife. They lived on the edge of town, and wished above anything else for a little boy. They prayed and prayed, and eventually God answered their prayers, and they were blessed with a little boy whom they named David."

"Maybe it's Jewish," Alex said. "David is a Jewish name."

"I always thought of it more as a Christian name," she said.

"Now David was a bright young lad who took to most things quickly," she said. "His father the carpenter began to teach him the ways of woodworking at a young age. He showed him how to use a hammer, and how to soak a wooden beam so it could be shaped by stone weights cantilevered over a fulcrum, and how to drive a wooden peg if nails were lacking, so that it would hold. David's father was a carpenter of bridges and houses, and he showed David as he grew up how to build and bend and mend.

"David did well as a carpenter, as he had his father's skill and his mother's care for doing something right. His apprenticeship was coming along fine, and on his birthday in his eighteenth year, his father took him into town to the tavern to celebrate.

"It so happened that a band of gypsies was traveling through town then, and they were playing at the tavern for coppers and pennies. The gypsies generally weren't allowed in those parts, but at the tavern they were considered a cheap source of entertainment, and given lodging for a small fee."

"You're not supposed to call them gypsies anymore, you know," he said. "It's not p.c."

"That's how the story was told to me," she said.

"As soon as David heard the gypsies play, he fell in love. For one purple-eyed gypsy girl played a beautiful harp of red cedar wood, and she played it so liltingly, so lovingly, that David was lost. That harp could sigh a soft lullaby one moment, and the next cut a jig so sharp even the old men would stand and tap out a few steps. It could wax wobbly about lost love or strum out a brisk marching tune, and David was rapt by every delicate note.

"That night he stole away with the gypsies. Their wagon wheel needed to be fixed, and in exchange for an hour of skilled hammering they gave him passage to the next town. On the way he pleaded with the purple-eyed gypsy girl to teach him the harp.

"She tried as best she could, but David's thick, calloused fingers didn't seem made for the delicate work. Try as he might, David could only pluck out the simplest of tunes. He cursed his lack of experience and pleaded with the gypsies to teach him as long as it took to master the harp. In exchange, he promised them, he would mend their wagon whenever it broke down. The gypsies agreed, as their wagon was very old and broke down quite often.

"Every day the gypsies would travel to a new town, and every evening David would listen as the purple-eyed gypsy girl played beautifully on that rose-colored harp. And every morning he would practice as the purple-eyed gypsy girl slept, slowly improving. He would fall asleep exhausted, briefly dozing from midafternoon till evening, and dream about the beautiful sounds he would someday play, lovely music he could hear swelling in his dreams.

"Years went by. As the seasons passed, David's improvement at playing the harp slowed, then stopped. David had neither the skill nor the dexterity to play the harp as well as he had dreamt. He had reached his natural limit. Slowly, painfully, David had a revelation. He realized that if he played for the rest of his life, he would not get any better, and that the music that he heard in his heart and wished for and loved would be forever out of his reach to produce."

Alex turned to look at Alyssa in the dark.

"What happened after that?" he said.

"That's all of the story I remember," she said.

"You just made that up right now, didn't you?"

"What do you think?"

"I think it's stupid," Alex said.

"Alright."

Alex paused, waiting for Alyssa to respond.
"I know what you're trying to say," he said.
"What am I trying to say?"
Alex didn't answer.

How About This

An old man, life passed, it's all behind him. He's retired. He used to be a shoe salesman. Never married, no kids. He goes about his life at the retirement home with a certain dejected fumbling.

He meets a boy, a young kid. The boy is helping out at the retirement home. The boy is a typical white middle-class crew-cut kid. They hit it off; old man is happy, boy is happy, the end.

Of course it doesn't end there. Of course.

Start with a lonely man, a businessman; it's cold, it's winter. He goes to the movies by himself, doesn't know many people outside his family. He always can feel an immense gulf between himself and others.

How to describe it?

He is amazed how little one can possibly know about anybody else. He's happily married, he has kids, it is all well and good. But he has no illusions. He knows he doesn't fully understand his wife, that he can never truly understand his life. He can only form the barest outline of a theory as to how things should go, how they might behave, but then some glaring fact contradicts this and he has to scrap the whole system. He's been doing this his whole life. It's exhausting. Every so often he throws up his mental hands and says, "Enough! Just let it be."

But then something jogs his interest, and he can't help but ponder again. Over and over; it's a picture of neurotic repetition. Because he can never fully understand others, he feels a distance. The distance itself doesn't bother him as much as it once did. That he has come to take for granted.

No, what disturbs him most is the fear that he is the only one who feels this gulf. The idea that there could be others who don't, who either somehow bridge the gap or are unaware that a gap exists at all, that thought above all else leaves him anxious and desperate.

So he goes to the movies. He always makes sure that whatever movie he sees has been proclaimed popular by the press. He likes movies with splendid stars and predictable story lines. There, alone in the darkness, he feels a measure of control, a measure of empathy. There isn't any space between him and the characters in the movies. If there is danger, the hero is frightened but resolute. If there is nudity, the hero is calm and collected. It is a system; there is order.

I used to have this problem with sleep. There's no other way to describe it. I didn't sleep for months; I'd lay awake at night and stare at my clock, watching its bright red LEDs shine upon the corner of my room. I'd always be dead tired, until finally I'd fall asleep at seven o'clock, just in time to wake up a few hours later and drag myself through my day.

To be honest, it's not so bad; you're so tired all the time you don't notice if things aren't going so well. When you've only had two hours of sleep, it's hard to really care about anything.

Sometimes I'd dream. But the dreams would never get very far. I'd always wake from the heat or some other damn thing. All night long, a malignant pain or a recurrent thought would jolt me to consciousness, and I'd struggle befuddled, groping for sentience. Where the dreams ended and my waking life began became confused. The dreams would never finish; sometimes it wasn't even clear when they began. It was horrible, not to really dream. Often I would remember only splintered fragments.

Another man is dead inside. He is a computer repairman. He's the one you call when the server goes down. He has a full tool set and a keen mind. But his conversation skills are lacking. Maybe it's because he never really connects with his clients. His job doesn't give him much opportunity to talk to anybody. When he does speak, it is usually in response to a technical question, or comments on the weather; it's all part of a service. His dispatcher calls him up and says a certain client, a certain customer, needs a repair.

So he drives on out to the company. It's any company anywhere. His favorite part of the job is when he arrives, and he has to find the secretary who shows him what the problem is. He gives a big old smile; he likes it when the secretaries are women. They used to all be women; now only maybe 70 percent are women, and they are called administrative assistants. Somehow they seem to have gotten older. He likes the beginnings most because then there is always the hope that there will be something there. There is always the potential. This is what he lives for.

One time, he was looking for a corporation out in the country. He'd been driving for an hour, and he wound up at a house. A large Victorian house, painted bright purple, with yellow trim. He was amazed. He'd checked the address twice; it was right. This was the place. But what was he to do? It looked too comfortable to possibly be a serious place of business (especially one with a Linux server with a broken tape drive). He imagined going up to the house and trying to explain what he was doing there.

The front door opened. A woman in a blue dress with little white flowers on it and a pink apron stepped out. She absently rubbed her hands on the front of her apron and smiled grandly. He thought he could smell oatmeal cookies baking. She waved to him to come on in, that sure, this was the place, he'd found it all right. Welcome.

Nothing was going right for Julie. Her brand new braces made her teeth ache constantly. She couldn't eat any hard food. Strange pimply sores were appearing all over her face and body. On top of that, she'd just moved, and it was her freshman year in a brand new high school. All this conspired together to make her feel like shit every day.

And Mark didn't help. He was this big bully on the bus who used to sit behind her and call her "dogface." She would move, but he'd just follow her; there were only a few people on the bus. Of course, he was quite a sight as well. He seemed to be perpetually leering, and his eyes were tight against his nose. He looked just like a human mule. Or an ass.

Every time she saw him coming, she would grab the end of her braid. As he began to harass her, she would tug. She would tug repeatedly until she could feel her scalp growing hot from the pain. The feeling of her hair almost ripping out of her head distracted her from his insults. She would just sit looking straight ahead, trying to ignore him behind her, tugging on her braid over and over and over and over.

A boy dreamed of emancipation. Not anything radical really; this was not slavery. He dreamed of freedom from worry, from pain, from boredom, from malaise. He'd dreamt these utopian thoughts even when he was young.

As a child, he pushed himself toward this goal. When he was ten, he climbed out on the roof from his sister's window. His older sister was shocked. They had been playing around, had opened the window and the screen, and peered way out down the three stories to the ground until she had gotten dizzy. She had pulled back, and suddenly the boy had been seized by the most peculiar sensation. He had ventured out onto the hot slate roof in the middle of summer. His sister let out a little shriek and made to grab him, but froze, afraid her movement might send him spinning down. He edged away from the window, ignoring her. It was a brave new world up here.

The slate was narrow and rather steep, but the pitch was gentle enough for him to get a good footing. He could look out upon all the other tall slate-roofed houses, and the tops of the trees. He could see for almost two city blocks in any direction.

He gently waddled his way to the edge of the roof and sat. He looked down. It seemed high, but not nearly as high as he'd imagined. He sat there looking down upon the bushes and the pavement until his sister, giving up on convincing him to come back by herself, yelled for their father, who somewhat heatedly insisted that the boy return inside immediately. This he did. He was soundly punished but could offer no explanation for his actions. He remembered thinking that this finally would rid him of his glum moods and boredom, of his occasional sadness and fits of anxiety. He had done something brave and challenging; surely this would settle his restless spirit.

But it did not. Later the boy tried many things. He worked hard at school, and when that didn't help, he didn't work hard at school, until finally his teachers and his parents gave up on him. He graduated from high school and moved out to an apartment and had a life. Finally, he thought, this independence will give me the backbone I need to figure things out.

Yet he was still plagued by the same problems, always troubled. He went back to school, got his teaching certificate, barely. He traveled. He journeyed on what meager money he had and tried to see how far away he could get. He saw Europe. He taught American kids in private schools in India. He had many wondrous experiences. He tried various religions. He thought that finally, perhaps, he would be cured.

He was sitting one day, meditating in a temple in a country where he didn't speak the language, when it occurred to him that things would never really get better. Or if they did get better, it was not going to be a sudden transformation, a spiritual splash of cold water that would wake him up to new ways of seeing and being. The boy finally figured that it would have to be a gradual change, that each tiny step might get him closer to something, and that he might never arrive, but that if things were to change at all, they would only do so very, very slowly.

21

I remember once seeing a girl with a coffee cup, leaning against an archway at the train station. She looked like she should have been begging, but she wasn't. She was right on the edge in terms of attire; she could either have been dressed as she was because she had to or because it was somehow trendy. There was a row of four guys alongside her asking for money with various explanatory signs, and there she was, just sitting, trying not to make eye contact, with a blue backpack and a cup of coffee. I had to look twice at the coffee; I thought it was her begging cup at first, but no, she was actually drinking coffee.

When I passed by the same spot some ten hours later, all the other people had gone. She was still there with her bag, holding herself to keep warm. Even in the middle of the summer the night is cold in New York. She didn't have the cup of coffee anymore; she was just looking around at the people going by. I guess the other homeless people had better places to go. I gave her a twenty.

I didn't know what I was doing until I'd already done it; if I'd thought about it more, I probably wouldn't have. She looked at me confused for a second; I was confused too. I didn't know whether I was assuming things or being kind. She said thank you and took it, and I nodded and hastened off before she could explain or ask me why I'd given it to her. I couldn't have told her if I'd wanted to.

What was her story? How did she end up there? What happened to her? Where had she been? Who was she? Where was she going?

They'd been hiking for an hour. Just an hour; they had ten days to go, if they hiked at a moderate pace. The Hundred Mile Wilderness in Maine was not quite what they'd expected. At least, not what she'd expected. They'd been hiking only an hour, and already she was having second thoughts.

It wasn't that either of them was tired. Henry was getting more energetic by the minute. Nora found it disturbing. The longer they walked, the more frantically he seemed to be reaching for things to say, for ways to entertain her. She tried to tell him to relax, but he wasn't listening to her. She gradually lapsed into silence; whenever she tried to talk, he would interrupt her with an edgy joke and this laugh that grew strained.

By the time they stopped at the first lean-to for the night, Henry was exhausted. She asked him what was wrong, what she could do. He just shook his head dumbly. They were both tired from the hike, but this was more than that. He avoided eye contact and mumbled he was tired. They ate their cold pasta in silence. Nora both cooked and cleaned the dishes, even though it went against their original agreement.

In the night they slept in separate sleeping bags on different sides of the tent. She had tried to talk to him, but he had simply rolled away from her. She decided they'd figure it out tomorrow, and tried to sleep.

In the thick darkness she woke to a peculiar sound. She thought she heard him crying. It was odd. Here was Henry, big Henry, crying softly in the middle of the night. She reached out to him blindly. She wanted to comfort him. When her hand touched his shoulder, he stopped abruptly. She heard him turn toward her. She felt the cool wetness of his tears on her hand.

She pulled him close to her, and in the darkness they kissed. He cried a bit longer. She held him for awhile, and then they both fell asleep.

And the next day they were fine.

What would I think about as I lay awake at night? Oh, different things.

Sometimes I'd stare out the window at a street light that drooped over the sidewalk by my window. I'd watch the shades breathe with the wind, dampening and brightening in the reflected phosphorescent light. Street lights at night are always strange; phosphorescent lamps emit a certain near light that turns everything into thin carbon copies of the real world.

People look sickly and pale beneath it; nobody has any substance. They always float past the yellow pools of light from darkness into darkness, a brief glimpse of some passing emotion, some troubled look, and then they're gone.

And then, of course, there is the curious story of Guinness Fick. Guinness was named after that great book of books, that hallowed volume that documented his mother's greatest accomplishment. In her youth, Miss Heidi Fick had challenged herself to grow the longest hair in the world. And that was what she did. It took sixteen years of her life; from when she was fourteen until she was thirty, she never cut her hair. Every morning she would braid her hair, then roll it into a big ball stored in a bag behind her head. The weight alone gave her neck cramps. Finally, after sixteen years, she was ready. When she did unroll her hair for the Guinness judges, it was sixteen feet five inches long. This beat the previous record by a good three inches. This was Heidi's sole claim to fame, her one and only crowning achievement, for which she hoped to be eternally remembered. Thus, she named her only child Guinness.

When Guinness was twenty-four, he fell in love. It was a girl who worked at the same bottling plant as he. They were engaged. But eventually he had to end it because her name was Hicki Ledermeyer. The fact that her married name would be Hicki Fick was too much for Guinness. To top it off, when they were rhapsodizing about what to name their future child, she had insisted upon the name Nick if it was a boy. Not Nicholas, mind you, but explicitly Nick. Finally, when she pressured Guinness into giving a straight answer about their wedding date, he couldn't stand the thought of it all any longer, broke off the engagement, and moved to Iowa.

I don't know. I keep talking and talking. I feel I am wearing myself thin. I read once that the hull of the *Apollo* spacecraft, the one that went to the moon, was so thin the astronauts were afraid that if they pushed on it too hard with their feet it would break. I imagine them spiraling through the stars and moonlight in the night, afraid to move.

A young woman in L.A. had a normal life. This was the great tragedy, the great fault. She went to high school, fell in love, and then graduated. She went to Princeton, met her soon-to-be-husband, Frederick, moved out to L.A. Frederick was in advertising and was moderately successful.

They grew children in the suburbs. She did most of the raising of the kids, but she didn't mind. The Cleaver flashbacks subsided after a few years.

There were the occasional fights and squabbles. One time Frederick cheated on her. He moved out for almost three months, until she forgave him. Then there was the time little Jimmy smoked pot and got caught; he was grounded for half a year. He eventually went to Vassar.

When little Jimmy and Cindy were out of college and having children of their own, Frederick decided that Florida would be good for them. It had cheaper housing, and they didn't understand the young people who lived out in L.A. anymore. So they moved.

Frederick eventually died from a heart attack on a golf course, at the ripe old age of seventy-three. He had lived a full life. He was on the seventeenth hole and had been shooting one of the best games of his life.

Now the old woman spent a few years meandering around Florida. The kids called every Easter and Christmas but never visited. They didn't have time; Jimmy was in advertising too now. It was all quite exciting, just like his father.

The woman idled around, playing cards with her friends. That was the big attraction, playing cards.

One beautiful weekend the old woman decided to go out to the beach. She caught a bus. At the last stop, she cautiously stepped out into blazing heat. She walked out onto the sand. She felt the cool breeze of the ocean. She took off her shoes and waddled out into the surf. Her bare feet prickled in the gritty sand. The water was joltingly cold. She hiked up the dress she was wearing to avoid getting the fringe wet.

She looked out at the distance. The horizon was a thin, sinuous line. There was a palpable sense of the distance over broad water as she stared out into the emptiness. She wondered what came next.

All the other kids had gone inside. They had been playing hide-and-seek. Freddy wasn't done hiding. He was safe behind the big tree. Nobody had found him. That's because he was so quiet, and because he'd curled up into a ball so small that nobody could see him. He stayed out, even after all the other kids had gone inside. He knew he'd probably get in trouble, but it wouldn't be so bad.

He waited awhile behind the tree, but nobody came to get him. Eventually he came out from his hiding place with an exasperated sigh. He hesitantly stood out in the open, as if to say, "Here I am! Come get me!" But still no one came. He looked through the class window and saw his whole class inside, looking bored. They hadn't noticed that he was missing.

He lay down in the cool grass and closed his eyes. He thought that maybe if he just lay there real quiet nobody would ever notice him. He'd become invisible. He lay very still. He tried not to breathe. He tried not to think. If he just tried hard enough, everything could be still. He concentrated very hard.

One night I gave up on sleep. I'd watched the moon come and go and the sky brighten painfully. It was still dark when I slipped out into the city.

When you're tired enough, you keep going on the feeling of a certain lack of control, a certain high derived solely from being too weary to think straight. You seem caught perpetually on the edge of full consciousness; the result is that you feel like you're never completely there. You have to be careful because if you close your eyes, you have no sense of balance and might tip over.

As I walked, the streets felt hard. The "desert of the real" feels very palpable at five o'clock in the morning. I looked around for a vantage point from which to watch the sunrise. Suddenly a blinding glimmer from a mirrored building caught me.

The sun hit each mirrored window at once with a single blaze of light. Each window mirrored the same dazzling reflection, a thousand images of rising fire, all simultaneously bursting to life.

Dinner with Caitlin McRay

She worked beside me, her thin forearms caked with flour up to her elbows. Her slim fingers worked the dough over in smooth folds. She paused and wiped sweat from her forehead with her shoulder, careful not to get any flour on her face. She saw me looking at her. She gave me a coy little smile, and I wondered, not for the first time, what my girlfriend would think about all this.

While she worked on the dough, I was making the sauce. Canned tomato, fresh tomato, some crushed garlic sautéed in olive oil with onions. Basil. Fresh peppers. It was my first time actually making homemade sauce. It was my first time cooking anything, really, without someone else directing the whole thing.

Caitlin flattened the dough into one thin layer and began to slice it into fine strips no thicker than her pinky. She repeated the process until the dough was just the right size for fettuccine. She was meticulous.

"Caitlin McRay, please."

The receptionist typed the name into her computer. She shook her head.

"I'm sorry, I can't find her."

I nodded, and looked around the hospital uncomfortably. The reception area looked empty. The receptionist hadn't checked the eating disorders ward; I could see a special separate list from where I was standing in front of the counter. I didn't want to have to say it out loud.

"She has an eating disorder."

The receptionist raised her eyebrows and made an "oh" with her mouth in understanding. She checked the other list, and oh yes, it turns out she is here.

"Fifth floor, down on the left. Follow the directions on the door when you get there."

I thanked her and took the elevator up.

The sign on the door read, "Access to the E.D.S. ward is available by appointment only. Please pick up the phone and wait to be buzzed in."

When I picked up the phone, the other side of the line rang once before someone answered it.

"Yes?"

"Yes, I'm Ryan DeNilo."

"And whom are you here to see?"

"Caitlin McRay."

They buzzed the door open, and I padded down the hall, looking for the door with her name on it. There seemed to be a peculiar sort of odor, something rancid, thinly covered by the smell of disinfectant. It reminded me of the geriatric ward where I had visited my grandfather after his first heart attack. Previously I'd only associated it with bedpans and the incontinent.

The only people around were young girls. Very thin young girls. Too thin; some were showing bone, and I had flashes of concentration camps. I tried not to make eye contact with anyone. I found Caitlin's room down on the right.

She was lying back in bed with tubes in her arm, propped up by a pillow and looking rather thin and pale. She said hi and gave me a weak smile. I gave her a hug.

"Here, I brought you some stuff."

I produced a package of junk I'd found around my apartment before catching the bus out to the hospital. She smiled at me, flattered.

"Ryan, you didn't have to do that."

"I know," I said. I dropped the package on the bed, and she opened the bag and brought out each item gingerly.

A deck of cards (to play solitaire), one of the *Harry Potter* books (not the new one, the first in the series), some crayons and paper. Gifts you'd give a kid, not a twenty-year-old woman. She seemed happy to have them.

"They're perfect for me in here," she said. "I have lots of time on my hands."

"That's what I figured."

I forced a smile. She may have been thinner than usual. I don't know. It was hard to tell. Her five-foot-six frame was always thin; I think maybe it was her Polish roots. Her hair was thin and stringy, blonde and brown strands pulled back behind her ears, her brown eyes quietly looking out at me. Her skin was pale, but not paler than normal. She'd always had freckles. I thought she looked fine, though I suppose it's not one of those things you can tell just by looking at her.

She had a small cut at the left corner of her lip. I asked her if it was a cold sore. She said it wasn't.

"It's from purging."

"Beg your pardon?"

"Purging. It's what they call it when you, you know, throw up."

I tried to act like this was normal. She said she got the cut from purging so much that the side of her lip cracked, and then scabbed over.

I felt like taking my hand and rubbing it against her face as if I were roughly applying sunblock to a child. I wanted to hold her head still with my left hand and with my right scrape the scab off, leaving a clean wound.

I was at work when she told me. I'd just finished making a banana split for this fat lady when Derrick, the guy I work with, said that there was a call for me. I wiped the chocolate sauce off my hands into the damp towel that I'd laced through my belt loop and took it.

"Yeah?"

"Hey, Ryan. It's Caitlin."

"Hey, Caitlin. Where were you last night?"

We were supposed to go to a movie. She had bailed on me. I'd waited over an hour outside the theater, holding the tickets.

31

Dinner with Caitlin McRay

"I'm sorry, I couldn't make it."

"Well what happened?"

I was eyeing the customers. A black woman with two kids was giving Derrick a hard time because she said he hadn't put enough chocolate sauce on her kids' sundaes. The youngest she held against her hip, while the older boy was jumping up and down with a spoon in his mouth.

"I'm in the hospital."

"What happened?"

The older boy let out a scream of frustration and jabbed the air with his spoon. I wondered why we let people bring kids in here in the first place.

"I fainted yesterday, Ryan."

"Are you okay? What happened? Are you sick?"

Derrick took care of them as best he could and moved on down the line. I watched the family move over to a table. The young boy jammed his spoon into the sundae, and spread chocolate sauce all over his face. His mother wailed. I had two hours left in my shift.

"Ryan, I'm bulimic."

Derrick was trying his best to manage alone. A haughty woman ordered a nonfat vanilla frozen yogurt in a dish, and I could feel him getting frustrated. Even the way she handed over the money was irritating.

It occurred to me that I should find something to say.

"Well, that explains the food thing. I was always amazed at how much you could eat. And not gain weight."

The joke wasn't really funny, and she didn't laugh.

I imagined she was waiting at some pay phone in the hospital, choosing to call me over everyone else. In my mind's eye, she was holding the phone, trying to keep it together, trying her best not to cry. I wanted to act like I wasn't too fazed, and somehow come off as nonchalant. What I said to her right now might be very important.

"Which hospital? I'll come visit you."

I should have known before she told me. In her bedroom there would be stacks of food in little piles. She would hoard it weirdly, stuffing bagels in drawers, leaving salads out until the lettuce changed color and the dressing congealed. It was all a horrible waste.

And she would eat and eat but not gain weight. It seems kind of silly, how incredulous I was that such a thin little thing could pack away all that food. When you look at it now, of course she had a problem. Of course that was the most obvious explanation. But back then I thought that she just had a fast metabolism, thin from birth. Like she couldn't even gain weight if she tried.

"Why do you do it?"

"Do what?"

"Take care of her. Visit her. I mean, I know you're her friend and all. But she's not your responsibility."

I rolled away from Sarah and looked at the wall.

"Are you jealous?" I asked.

"It's not like that."

In the dark I could hear her voice becoming petulant.

"I know," I said.

Still, I could understand if she were. I'd gone out to visit Caitlin a couple times a week for the last month. Twice had been on the weekends, when Sarah and I could have been doing something.

"You do spend a lot of time with her."

I could feel Sarah's rage next to me in bed in her stiff motion and tense muscles. We'd been going out three months, and things had been going well before this. I tried to understand, but I was already too tired. I'd spent the whole day in the hospital with Caitlin, trying my best to be a good friend, giving advice, holding her while she cried. And today was my only day off. I was not up to trying to cope with any more problems.

I rolled toward her and made an attempt. Her red hair fell about her tanned face, but she stared straight at me. She looked like she was trying not to be upset.

"She's my friend," I said.

"She could go to somebody else."

"There is nobody else."

"What about her family? Her other friends?"

I turned away from her. She seemed about to cry.

I closed my eyes.

"They're not here," I said. And we left it at that.

I met her parents once. Nice folks. They came all the way out from Texas to visit. Her father worked for a mutual fund company in Austin. He gave me an amiable handshake that was kind of limp, and a smile that was all teeth. Her mother seemed like an addendum to her father. She held her purse in front of herself with both hands and smiled hesitantly. Caitlin got special leave to go out to dinner with them when they came to visit. She was still in the hospital then. They asked her to invite all her friends so that they'd get a chance to meet them, so I went with Caitlin and her parents, just the four of us. We got Thai food.

Her mother seemed the quiet type. She would smile and ask polite questions. Where do you work? When did you meet Caitlin? I explained that I worked at Big Ed's Ice Cream Parlor and had met Caitlin her junior year in college. I was taking an extension school class that overlapped with her English classes, and she'd helped me out. She'd let me borrow her notes. Mrs. McRay nodded slower and slower, until she was just sitting in her chair in the Thai restaurant, trying to look like she was paying attention. After every question, she'd just sort of subside, then jostle herself and ask another question, like she was reading from a book and kept losing her place.

Caitlin's father seemed jovial enough, but always slightly apologetic for his wife. He would look over too quickly when she asked a question and always rephrase her sentences, as if what she said wasn't quite right and he just wanted to make sure I got her meaning. They talked to Caitlin comfortably, as if whatever problems she was having were normal and could be heroically taken in stride.

I understand why they didn't just take her home. It must have been expensive to visit, coming all the way from Texas, treating her to dinner. I'm sure they had their reasons for not taking care of her. They left when she was still in the hospital, and promised to help out with her rent on her apartment and the hospital bills. They seemed like fine people.

We played cards for an hour at her hospital bed. She didn't know any card games at all, so I taught her how to play solitaire, then Klondike. I showed her how to play poker, both five-card draw and stud, and explained to her how the betting worked. Then I showed her how to play gin rummy and we played a few hands.

She kept being distracted. Once someone flushed the toilet out in the hall, and she seemed to cringe. I asked what was wrong.

"Nothing. Somebody's going to get in trouble, though."

I picked up the stack and put down a two.

"Why?"

"We're not supposed to flush the toilet ourselves. One of the nurses always checks first."

She looked at the two and then hesitantly picked one up from the pile.

I fidgeted in my seat and tried to think of a new subject. Visiting times were almost over. They'd be serving dinner pretty soon, and though I might want to stick around, it lasted two hours.

"Why does dinner take so long anyway?" I asked.

She shrugged and threw down the ace of hearts.

"They like to talk about how important eating together is, and share stuff over dinner. It's a bonding thing. It helps us all cope. Eating is very nerve racking."

I picked up her ace and put down the eight of clubs.

"Is it hard?"

"What do you mean?"

"Is it hard eating with people?" It seemed a valid question.

"Yeah. But I have to eat sometime. It's better eating with people than without. I just wish it was people who I knew better." She seemed to make a point not to look at me, and took a card from the pile.

"I can come to dinner if you want."

She smiled and shook her head. She seemed to be trying to act with bravado, but it didn't come off right.

"No. I have to get permission before noon. It's too late now."

"Maybe some other time then."

"Yeah."

I tried to think about what I could do.

"We should do something when you get out."

She looked at me. She held her cards carefully, her hands close in to her stomach over the folded sheets.

"What do you mean?"

"Let's have dinner. We'll cook. Together. It will be fun. Just you and me. What do you think?"

She smiled at me hesitantly, and looked to the side. She seemed to be listening for something. She turned back to me.

"What will we make?" She said it as if she were teasing me.

"Let's make pasta. An old Italian recipe from my family. You'll love it. What do you say?"

She shrugged. "Okay. It'll be fun."

She laid down her cards.

"Gin."

From a pamphlet I read in the waiting room, waiting for visiting hours to begin:

"Diagnostic Criteria for Bulimia Nervosa:

Recurrent episodes of binge eating. An episode of binge eating is characterized by both of the following: first, eating, in a discrete period of time (e.g., within any 2-hour period), an amount of food that is definitely larger than most people would eat during a similar period of time and under similar circumstances; second, a sense of lack of control over eating during the episode (e.g., a feeling that one cannot stop eating or control what or how much one is eating).

Purging Type: During the current episode of Bulimia Nervosa, the person has regularly engaged in self-induced vomiting or the misuse of laxatives, diuretics, or enemas."

"It's a spoiled-little-girl disease."

"You don't know what you're talking about." We'd been waiting for my bus five minutes before Sarah started in again. I was already late for work, mostly because she'd given me a hard time ever since I'd woken up at her place. A tall guy in a suit and glasses looked at us, then away. I hoped Sarah didn't talk any more about it.

"Oh? Like twenty-four thousand people die every day from hunger. I looked it up. From malnutrition. From a lack of food. And you're going to tell me that Caitlin's voluntarily not eating isn't a symptom of her being a spoiled brat?"

"She's not anorexic, she's bulimic." I could feel the suit get all interested.

Sarah shook her head.

"Whatever. It's still something she can control. All those starving people, and she just hurts herself. And you. Why can't she just stop?"

I could see the bus coming.

"We never cook dinner together," she said.

"You never wanted to cook dinner together."

"How do you know? You never offered."

The bus pulled up to the curb.

"You never asked. I have to go," I said.

"You asked her. Why don't you offer to cook dinner with me?"

"You're not bulimic."

I figured if I played cards with her, if I talked to her, if I cared about her, then maybe. It's funny. Though I didn't know in the beginning, as long as I've known her she's been sick. You begin to wonder if you'd like them if they weren't sick. If their sickness is what keeps you there. Are you their friend who has stuck with them to help them through their sickness, or does their sickness make you their friend?

And she's on so many medications. Oftentimes I think I'm making her better, but I can't tell. She's so up and down. Once she was so happy to see me I was suspicious. I asked her what was different, even though I didn't really want to know the answer. And I was right. The truth of it was they'd just changed her medication.

We finished cooking and retreated from the stifling heat of the kitchen to sit in the backyard at a picnic table as the dusk came on. Neither of us wore shoes, and the grass against my bare feet felt soothing after the heat of the kitchen. The evening air was delicious.

It was a simple meal. We sat out on the rough brown wood and chatted idly about things. I could hear the clink of silverware and the murmur of conversation as every family in the neighborhood settled down to dinner.

I ate quickly, and went back in for seconds. When I came back, Caitlin was half finished with her food. She was eating slowly, as if immensely preoccupied. I tried to concentrate on being entertaining and talked about my day. I think she nodded and forced a nervous smile. Once we were done, I piled up the empty plates on the table, and we sat for a while.

The pasta sauce had dried by now and formed a thin film around the rims of the bowls.

I couldn't understand exactly what was wrong. I wanted to comfort her if I could. I tried to laugh it off, but I think that made it worse.

I could hear the families in the neighborhood picking up their dishes and washing their plates, scraping food down the drain. Looking at her sitting next to me, something moved between us, and I felt like I was losing her. I can hardly describe it; it was as if something horrible had happened, and we were pretending to ignore it, and she was just waiting until I left so she could cry. I didn't know what to say.

"Well, Ryan, it's time to go, probably. I'll do the dishes. Thanks for coming."

The evening was still quiet around us.

I looked away from her at the side of the house. I noticed one of the window shades was half drawn.

"Listen, Caitlin. Listen. I know...I mean, I can imagine..."

Half drawn like that, could someone see us from inside? Or could I see them?

"You just have to try. If you tried hard enough, you'd be better, believe me. And you'll be okay. Really. You just have to try. Can you do that, Caitlin? Please? Can you do that for me?"

She took the plates and went into the kitchen, and thanked me again, and said goodnight.

When I saw her the next day, she avoided making eye contact with me. She pretended nothing was wrong, that nothing had happened. Her mouth was cut fresh, a little glistening pink in the corner of her lip. She seemed dull and beyond me.

And I couldn't do anything.

Intermission: An Interview with the Editor

Interviewer: Thank you for taking the time to speak with me.

Editor: It was part of the agreement, wasn't it? Let's get on with it.

I: Why did you select *FYM [Frustrated Young Men]* as the first book from PulpLit Publishing?

E: We were desperate. We didn't know anyone else who would take a chance and publish their book with an unknown entity with little backing. When John came to us, we leapt at the chance.

I: How intimately were you involved in the editing of *FYM*?

E: Distantly. Once I'd make the selection, Rebecca [Hardiman] did most of the copyediting. I mostly edit the zine, PulpLit.com.

I: Let's talk about that. What makes your zine different from other zines?

E: Not much. I've been trying to move us more toward a niche. I want to bring on writers like [Heather] Havrilesky and Cary Tennis. Then we'd be in the "excellent writing" niche. But the publisher keeps saying "we have no money, are you crazy?" I'm trying to make something beautiful, put it out there for other people to enjoy. But I always get shot down.

I: Do you feel that you are a harsh editor?

E: Do you know where the term *editor* comes from?

I: No.

E: It's from the Latin *edere* which means to put forth. In Rome, in the Coliseum, the gladiators, they would occasionally live long enough to become famous. They would have posters put up, proclaiming that the great "Amenadeus," or whoever, was to battle a lion or some new challenger. They would call the person who designed, created, and put up the posters an *editor*. Editors originally were a group of people who intimately and directly benefited from the pain of other people. That is to say, editors were compensated because someone else's suffering was entertaining to the masses.

I: I didn't know that.

E: Yes. Those editors were harsh. I'm merely selective.

I: Well, do you feel that you're a particularly selective editor?

E: Yes. But that is an editor's job. An editor is supposed to act as a gatekeeper, in at least two distinct ways. One, they make sure that everything the reader sees has been thoroughly copyedited. But also, they make sure that the content is interesting, is thought provoking. If editors are doing a good job, they act as a filter, making sure that readers only get the best of what was available. That is what they're paid for. Or, in my case, not paid for.

I: What do you say to those who say that you're not qualified to be an editor, that you don't have enough experience?

E: No comment.

I: What do you look for in a submission?

E: Anything original that will really grab people. I don't care if it's highbrow, lowbrow, genre-fict[ion], whatever. It just needs to be compelling right from the first sentence. If you think editors are harsh, think about readers. They'll click to something else without a twinge. You have to really grab them.

I'd like to go back to your previous question. I don't know who has been saying that to you, but let me just say, I think I am qualified. And if they think that they can do a better job, let them start their own Web site. Okay, I just needed to respond to that.

I: Is there anything else you'd like to add?

E: Just this: aspiring writers shouldn't take rejection too seriously. All it means is that the editor may have been having a bad day, or didn't get to the good section of your piece, or needed something else to finish out the issue. I think far too often writers think that rejection is a judgment of their whole body of work. It's often not. It sometimes is, but it's often not.

Toby Grey

I don't think there is anything wrong with me, not really. But I suppose when you get therapy that must mean that you have some issues you need to address, so I'm willing to believe that others think that there may be something wrong with me. If you asked my psychiatrist, he would say that I was unbalanced, that perhaps I need some medication (which I refuse to take), or that I require longer therapy (though I barely tolerate the current dosage). Then he would scribble something in his notepad, perhaps a diagram showing how my id is kicking the shit out of my super ego, or vice versa.

I don't know about Dr. Faulk. I sometimes wonder if he is getting more from my therapy than I am. I know I'm not supposed to notice, but he seems to get oddly excited if I bring up something really perverse. Once I told him my thoughts on the *Cosby Show*, how all that nice wholesomeness just made me want to fuck Mrs. Huxtable. His theory is that I yearn for a more stable household environment. Really it's that Mrs. Huxtable is a nice piece of ass, but whatever. I could set him straight, but I don't want to give him any more grist for the mill. I can almost see the wheels in his head grinding already, trying to figure me out.

On the flip, his keen interest in "everything Toby" leads to a tendency to lie on my part, or at least to exaggerate. I find myself mentally storing all the perverse or antisocial thoughts that occur to me in a tight mental cage, so that I can drag them out, still kicking, and vivisect them in session. One must entertain one's audience, after all. If he knew how simple minded I really was, I think he'd rapidly lose interest. Whatever my parents are spending on this should be viewed as an investment; someday I will no doubt write a bestseller about Just How Fucked Up My Parents Really Are. I wouldn't want to tell them that, though. They're already worried enough.

I think they know things I've tried to keep secret, but they act like they don't know. Or more specifically, like they want me to know that they know, and that they're ignoring it on purpose, and that I should be thankful that they are ignoring it and not making a big deal about it. I suppose I am thankful, but I'm unsure whether I should be. Every time they say we have to have a "serious talk," my kidney dives into my stomach. I keep thinking they've finally found out that I've tried Ecstasy or that they heard about when I got so stoned that time, or something. I mean, I KNOW they know I smoke pot. I reek of it every time I come home. If they don't know, they're brain-dead or they lack a sense of smell. Or just don't care enough to notice.

My father is a professor. He seems to be not all there all the time. My mother works all the time. If I ruffle her she will focus on me and attack the problem like it's a presentation before a client. You should see her cook. The entrée hasn't a chance in hell. It's like a contact sport.

I'm not sure whether my father doesn't care or whether he's just too busy to deal. He reads all the time, which is basically his job description. He's a valuable resource in our household, like an encyclopedia. You only bring him into the conversation when you're curious about this or that fact, but not when you need an actual opinion. Ask him to opine on anything, and if the subject is more complex than whether we should have chicken or beef for dinner, he'll mumble something about Socrates and beef contributing to global warming.

You think I'm kidding, but I'm not. We asked him whether he wanted beef or chicken when my uncle was coming to visit, and he thought awhile, and pointed out that the third leading contribution to methane emissions behind cars and factories was cows, through the sheer quantity of their flatulence. An interesting fact that I suppose is relevant in one way of thinking, but my mother went with beef anyway, because she wanted to make this aggressive new recipe she'd seen in *Redbook*.

I'm beginning to wonder whether I'm living in the same reality as my parents. I mean, how could they go on and on with their daily lives if they had experienced such a thing as marijuana? How could they participate in normal conversation if they knew that they instead could be having oral sex? How is that possible?

Anyway, I ended up here because I didn't leave my room for twelve hours or so and my mom decided to be proactive and started doing research. She figures that therapy will be good for me, maybe because then she can get back to work and doesn't have to deal. My Dad has verified that, for 27 percent of the teenage population, therapy can do a lot of good.

Back to my third parent, Dr. Faulk. It's embarrassing that we have to pay to get someone to be my friend/adviser. I have a suspicion that he nods off mentally every once in awhile. After a long pause, he kind of wakes up from whatever pansies he has been prancing through, and does the standard shrink thing, which is to scramble frantically in his head for a question in response to what I last said. It's almost as if he's thinking about his car insurance, or his wife, or his kids, or his mistress, and suddenly realizes I've stopped droning on and on. He struggles briefly to recall what I said last, finds it, and formulates a response to it, repeating this method until I go on to what I REALLY think about that subject and he is safe to wonder about his sex life again. I do the same thing in math class.

As another point of criticism, I get the feeling that he's done less living than I have, if that makes any sense. I feel this would sound incredibly arrogant if I didn't think it were actually true (which I suppose only proves that I am truly arrogant). I don't know what demons he has had to live down, but I somehow doubt that they are the same ones I've had to cope with. He doesn't seem the type. Does he ever wonder whether taking fewer drugs would have given him a better placement on the PSATs his junior year? If instead of letting Bird convince him to do that one extra hit off the bong two months before the test he'd tried to ingest *another* 1,000 flash cards of esoteric vocabulary, he'd have placed better than a 650, and would eventually have had a more significant life?

Does he ever wonder if he's mentally unbalanced? Has he ever had someone else question his sanity, further validating his own fears? What sort of life trauma has he had to deal with? Does he feel like everything he touches turns to shit?

I have a feeling his angst, if he has any, is a kind of routine, sourceless cerebral type. I imagine he lies awake at night, tossing and turning, with immense questions like "What is the DIFFERENCE between objective and subjective reality?" or "What if there isn't a God?" —the kind of metaphysical bullshit that I imagine you mentally masturbate to in college. Most of the time those kinds of things don't matter even to the person who poses the question, unless they're stoned. In which case *everything* sounds really deep.

All that said and done, he has helped me some. There's nothing like a shrink to make plain that you could be doing better things with your time, that your old ways of thinking could be exactly what's bringing you down in the end. This is a significant insight. If you could only change your thought patterns, look at the bright side, etc., maybe you wouldn't be so miserable all the time. The question is how to do that, especially when your inner moppet seems to be full of cynicism and self-derision.

"Tobias, how do you feel today?"

Dr. Martin Faulk is looking at me quizzically. I shrug, and he uncrosses his legs. As he waits, he recrosses his legs and doodles stick figures on his notepad.

"I feel like shit," I answer uncomfortably, and try to mimic his body posture. I think it makes him more comfortable when I act like him.

"Why do you say you feel like shit?"

I can shrug and look around his office for as long as I like, so I do. He intently studies my actions, or at least pretends to. I can't tell the difference.

For the well-adjusted, I should describe a shrink's office. I've been in three so far, and they all have the same feel. In the waiting room, they generally pipe in classical music from the radio. The coffee tables have interesting but in-offensive magazines, as well as very particular children's books, like "Mommy and Daddy Are Getting Divorced, Do They Still Love Me?" And perhaps puzzles that are not overly difficult, like those finger puzzles with the blocks, but nothing that will give a kid a self-esteem problem if he can't solve it. The architecture of the building seems to be kind of cheap, because usually it's an extension the shrink built onto his own house, so he pinched every penny he could to get it done. And the art is always kind of soothing too, either vaguely abstract Eastern stuff (a foggy landscape done in ink) or really simple pop art. Nothing anyone can overassociate with.

Within the womb, it generally looks like a normal office, sans any sharp objects. There's a desk I don't think anyone has ever done any work on, a couch, and sometimes, if the shrink has a sense of humor, a picture of Freud.

I always sit in the comfy chair, and my shrink sits across from me in another, more stern, chair. He seems very into his role as Doctor. He always wears his glasses, which I suspect he may not need, and he always wears sweaters, which I suppose I could psychoanalyze if I were bored enough. The current shrink is kind of a squat little guy, but he has promise. The first one wanted to put me on a "trial dosage" of Prozac for a month after a ten-minute interview, and the second kept on asking me questions about whether I had guilt about loving my mother. I didn't, and he seemed incredibly disappointed.

This third one, Dr. Martin Faulk, at least really talks to me, though only in a strange, dancing-around-the-point shrink kind of way. Our conversations usually go something like this:

Doc: So how are we doing today, Tobias?

Me: So, I've been having trouble sleeping again.

Doc: Why do you say you have been having trouble sleeping again?

Me: Uh, cause I have.

Doc: Last session we were talking about your future plans. Do they have anything to do with your trouble sleeping?

Me: What plans? I'm largely planless at this point.

Doc: Do you think your lack of plans may have to do with your problems sleeping?

Me: I don't know. Maybe.

Doc: What makes you believe that they do?

Me: Hell, I don't know, *you* said it.

Doc: Can you elaborate on that?

Me: On what?

Doc: Is it because of the people you hang around with that you say "on what"?

Me: What were we talking about again?

And on and on. He tries, though. Sometimes I think we've made some real progress. We both agree that the Red Sox are never going to win the World Series until they make some sort of official sacrifice, preferably a newborn lamb, like in the Bible.

The worst thing about being with my shrink is that I'm really edgy. He keeps on making me try to relax, I presume because he thinks I am having trouble "opening up," like I am a delicate flower, reticent before the loving bee (let's not look at that metaphor too closely). I suspect a far more mundane explanation. After about five minutes in that office, I'm dying for a cigarette.

I suppose now is as good a time as any to tell you about Jen. She was the size two 150 IQ. We first met at one of Rich's parties. Leave it to her to wear an evening dress to a kegger.

This particular party was rather tame by Rich's standards; the pot was not ubiquitous or central to the whole affair, but more peripheral than usual. Usually, Rich was the best guy to get hooked up; for a guy who usually wore pressed shirts, he was both a good supplier and a dedicated consumer. He had his own small house on his parents' sprawling property out on the edge of Ashburton. He'd moved into the guest-house when he turned sixteen, though it was unclear whether it was his choice or whether his parents had kicked him out of the main house. His parents basically left him completely alone to do his own thing, which made him one of the luckiest kids in my high school.

As a result, he had the wildest parties and would grow it in his own hydroponics in a small sealed-off heated greenhouse on the second floor. I have many fond memories of kicking up my feet and listening to him pontificate about how we all should live like him, that humans were evolved to be completely independent by their teens, that in some cultures fourteen-year-olds were having kids of their own and leading war councils, etc., etc. Total PBS bullshit.

I was moderately buzzed myself on a mixture of pot and beer, wearing my backward baseball cap in full townie garb, trying to fit in with the upper-crust folks who come to Rich's parties. Somewhere along the line I'd lost track of Bird, and was trying to find him when I ran into her on the stairs. Right then she was talking up Samantha from Chem class like they knew each other. Sam was looking around desperately, somewhat panicked. Sam was one of those uptight turtleneck girls who was destined for Radcliffe or Vassar.

Jen was gesturing rapidly with the cup and talking about the snowflake fallacy as if it were a conspiracy, saying that each snowflake being unique was a damn lie, like that old line that there is only one person to love in the whole world, and that neither made sense in a really rational scientific view of the world.

"If you want to say that the chances are low, okay. But to say that the chances are one in a thousand doesn't make it impossible. Saying no two are alike, that's like imposing some view of God or fate or some other bullshit on people, but subliminally, under the guise of science," she said, spilling beer on Rich's built-in-stair's carpet.

Sam saw me and pulled me over as a human shield.

"Jen, have you met Toby? Toby, Jen was just telling me about snow."

I extended my hand, all nervous and sweaty.

"Charmed."

"Totally," Jen said, taking my hand limply and bobbing her head somewhat wildly. Her eyes were glassy in a strangely attractive sort of way, probably a Pavlovian thing I picked up by watching one too many drugged-out porn stars on the Internet.

The only thing I can remember from the rest of that conversation is that I continued sweating and was trying desperately not to fuck up. Jen was glowing with panacea potential, her angular cheekbones counter accentuating her lips, her angelic face riding above a wiry frame that I was already fantasizing about.

We ended up outside, shivering as she slowly held a handful of snow up to her eyes and examined it to see if any of the snowflakes matched. I suggested that we go back inside because it was fucking freezing, and she laughed and threw the snow in my face. I was just drunk enough to take this as an invitation and tackled her into the snow.

When we toppled, she laughed and grabbed onto me, shivering too, her frigid hands dancing around the neck of my shirt trying to find my skin. I drew back, and she wriggled out and started walking away into the night, onto Rich's parents' property. I had a joint Bird had rolled, one of two we'd planned on book ending the party with, but as I said, I'd lost Bird when we'd arrived, so I figured what the hell. Jen made cooing noises when I pulled it out, so we smoked as we walked, crunching holes in the thin layer of ice over the snow.

There was a full moon and crisp, clean stars, with black oaks stretching bare tendrils up, dark against deep blue. I was feeling frosty, fuzzy, and witty. She seemed to be content, a little secret smile winking across her face in the dark.

I put my arm around her.

"Tell me you love me," she said. Her eyes caught mine steadily before sliding away, and I felt my spleen do mean things to my other internal organs.

"I love you," I said.

"You're full of it," she said.

"No."

"How could you love me?"

"Let's not talk about it."

She tilted her head back, her eyes closed, as if she was drunk.

"You may kiss me now."

And I thought that she'd spoiled it then, by saying it out loud like that, but went in to kiss her anyway.

But she hadn't, and I forgot myself for a second.

"I love you," I said.

"You're a romantic," she said.

"I love you," I said again. And it was true.

I should probably define my terms.

"Panacea potential" is this fantasy I have that I will meet this girl who will solve all my problems, that my happiness will waltz in the door in the form of some goddess with a 150 IQ, zero conceit, and a size two body. This fantasy itself, while a charming distraction, has spawned two of its own problems. First, that *every* girl has serious panacea potential until I actually get to know her. Then she is instantly degraded to mere mortal, leading to disappointment. Second, when I'm actually going out with a girl, every OTHER girl has this quality. Maybe not *every* girl exactly. Let's say one in three, and one in two at parties. Both of these factors put a serious damper on having any sort of stable relationship, or, even more disheartening, a consistent source of sex.

This delusion has persisted throughout most of my time at Ashburton High. I'll go out with a girl for about a month, and then she becomes a drag I am hoping to unload with as little bloodletting as possible. I have immense guilt about the whole thing.

I visualize this as a cycle, sort of a tight WWII-style-biplane tailspin. Every time I find a girl that is in any way cute and is willing to go out/service me, she will eventually disappoint. I become more depressed. Hence, I feel a need for that omnipotent fix more than ever, which leads to my hopes being even higher on the next girl. When she disappoints me, I sink even lower, and I do it all again and again. I don't suppose it's a horribly original thought; I probably read it in some magazine.

But even though I am aware of my behavior, I find myself incapable of changing it. I am like some deranged robot, who, upon reading the directions on the back of a shampoo bottle, has to interminably wash, rinse, and repeat, until my hair is shiny new and I collapse from exhaustion, my over watered body a big pruny mess.

The thing is, the thing that seems to make the whole world that much more infinitely complex, is that I do love them. I loved them all. It's not that I didn't think they were good enough, or even that I thought I wasn't good enough. It's like it is all just some dream, and the reality is that I am single and alone. As much as I do enjoy going out with one girl or another, I treat it more like it's a movie, where there's a certain script that has to be adhered to, like this was supposed to be a tragedy, damnit, and I didn't really have a choice. *Eventually*, it had to crash and burn. And all I could do was enjoy it while it lasted. And maybe try to get a little nook.

"Why do you say that you feel like shit, Tobias?"

Dr. Faulk always calls me Tobias. I haven't told him to call me Toby like everyone else because I know he would look into that somehow.

"I don't know."

I suddenly feel very tired. What does it matter, really?

Martin is looking keenly at me through bespectacled eyes. He looks concerned in that professional shrink sort of way.

"Do you want to elaborate on that?"

"No."

I itch. Can you ask to take a smoke break in the middle of a session?

"Whenever you're ready. We can talk about anything you want. Last session you mentioned that you felt guilty."

He flips the top sheet of his yellow notepad up, supposedly to read the notes from last session. I can read, upside down, something that looks like "depressive," and "may be displaying suicidal tendencies." This makes me feel kind of cool.

"You felt as if you had a 'pain in your chest,' like someone was 'twisting a knife around.' You also said you felt guilty. When did you first start to feel guilty?"

I wonder if he could be any more circumspect and still exert such acute pressure.

"You're talking about Jen, right?"

He adjusts his glasses and stares at me keenly. He looks like a man who has to amputate and, while he's looking forward to the challenge, worries that the patient may struggle.

"We can talk about Jen if you want."

"Let's not."

He just sits there and waits.

Sometimes he makes me feel kind of stupid.

Those first weeks back in school after winter break were fun, what with the furtive note passing in math class and quick kisses in the corners. I learned more about her; it's nice to be on the easy part of the learning curve.

Her father was a diplomat for Chile, or used to be. She said that he was looking for his next project now, but to me he looked like he was mostly taking it easy. Her mother had died some time ago. She didn't talk about it much.

To be perfectly honest, I have a hard time remembering the facts and figures. What more strobes through my mind is the smell of her hair. The curve of her neck. The way she would whisper quietly sometimes to herself, which I found creepy the first couple of weeks but then grew to like.

Our first date I picked her up in my mother's Land Rover and parked in the circular driveway. I'm all dolled up, of course: polo shirt and tight pants. I pull up to this big old house over in the rich part of Hayward, just five minutes late. It's one of those old wood-and-brick jobs that shine out bright like a city upon a hill, and you have to *hike* to get to the front door.

Her father answered my knock. He looked like a diplomat, which somehow translates in my mind to being faintly British. He had white hair and was wearing these rimmed glasses, and he had this big false grin. He introduced himself as Mr. Porter and called me Toby and invited me in. I realized I was underdressed.

He was wearing one of those sweaters, and the carpet gave some when I stepped on it, my sneakers sinking in. I saw a grandfather clock and a chandelier, along with a lot of shiny wood, and Jen descending the staircase. She was wearing one of those Jackie O. jackets — blue, with the fuzzy stuff around the cuffs and neckline, and a muff that looked like it was made from real fur. She had a short matching blue dress and a secretive little smile.

Dinner was nothing. I can barely remember the restaurant, only that it cost more than I make in a week working at the 7-Eleven and was one of those places where you've got to live up to the expectations of your waiter. Jen told me about Europe, and politics, and existentialism, and postmodernism, and I noticed her eyelids sparkled with these silver flecks in purple eye shadow. She seemed quite the literate chick. She would go a mile a minute, talking about Chomsky and Richter and Sartre all at once, her words bounding back and forth as she danced her fork over her linguine. I remember she didn't eat much dinner but finished off a monster piece of chocolate cake for dessert.

Now you may be wondering why such a smart girl hung out with such a dim bulb like myself. Part of it probably was the drugs. I found out that night that she liked to take caffeine pills and had recently graduated to amphetamines at Rich's aforementioned party, which explained her manic behavior that night.

She also liked pot, of which I was as good a supply as any. Rich was my source, which begs the question of why she didn't just cut out the middle man and go straight to Rich, which at least from an economic point of view would have made more sense. I suppose she liked the idea of slumming it.

After dinner we went up to the reservoir. It was Jen's crazy idea. I tactfully suggested we go make out in some woodsy corner, and she said that the reservoir was more romantic. I said "like how," and she said she'd show me. We pulled up, and I noticed one thing right off.

"It's fucking cold, Jen."

"Spoil sport."

She was looking away from me out the passenger side window at the moon. I could tell that I was going to be getting out of the car, just by her fanatic look, but figured I had to put up some resistance.

"They probably have guard dogs or something. They don't want people to poison the water supply. They probably have protection." I took a long drag and blew smoke out of my partially opened window. "Maybe motion sensors. And lights."

She unzipped her coat, tossed it in the driver's seat, took off her shoes, and got out. Her arms were goosebumped all over and pale in the moonlight. She immediately started shivering, and holding herself.

"You're going to catch your death," I said.

I got out of the car and went over to hold her, but she was already gone, stepping through wet grass with bare feet, briskly walking up the slope to the fence that enclosed the reservoir. I cursed my own weakness, and shut the passenger door. By the time I was done, she was already climbing the fence, her dress hiked up to her waist. I ran to catch up; when I reached the fence, out of breath, she was at the edge of the reservoir.

"Aren't you going to wait for me?" I said, in no particular hurry.

She didn't respond, and instead managed to unzip herself from the back. The dress whispered off her, revealed a black bra on white skin. Her back to me, shivering, she placed a tentative toe in the water.

"It's freezing!" she said.

I finished my cigarette, still on the other side of the fence.

"You're being crazy. Come back here. Seriously."

She laughed and dove in. I could see her limbs dance in and out of the black water. She began to swim a slow crawl across the surface. She turned to laugh at me again and took off her bra and panties, throwing them up on the edge of the reservoir. Then, kicking her legs up, she dove, her buttocks flashing out of the water before she disappeared beneath.

If there is a God, he must have poured all his notes and notions of sensuality, lust, and beauty into Jen. She was probably the most beautiful she would ever be. In my limited experience, sixteen to nineteen years old is the perfectly ripe peach of the female life cycle. Why do you think there are so many depraved examples of forty-five-year-old men dating barely legal girls, or strange college-to-high school relationships? I feel lucky to be among the hardy few who are also sixteen to nineteen, for whom society has not deemed it dastardly to admit that, yes, teenage girls are beautiful, and lovely, and amazing, and worthy of praise. They are young goddesses emerging, still in transition, before the jaded cynicism of their twenties has begun to make them "mature," sagging, purposeful, and chary.

Every curve of Jen's body is relentlessly etched in my mind, in my fingers, in my nerves. I can trace a thin line with my hand from the soft part between her toes up through smooth legs, the tiny lines behind her knees, the silk of her thigh up to a soft mount of fluffy hair, so light, so new to me.

Her small buttocks, firm and hard and thin, and around and around to a smoothly perfect belly button and thin depression before the approach to her ribs, and up to her glorious breasts, their hard nipples pink and tasting of metal.

I still dream about her, in an altered world, her thin arms wrapped around me, her fingernails digging into my back. I can feel my hands running up her back to hold her, her short-cropped blonde hair in curls, my fingertips massaging her neck as she nestles on top of me, my mouth and tongue biting gently into the smooth expanse of her neck, and we are making love again, her back arching.

It's just stupid now that I can't get her out of my mind. Her father got whatever appointment he was waiting on, and off they went to Washington after that semester. There was some gibbering and crying on my part, and she stroked my hair and said it was okay, and that we would talk. I told her I loved her.

After she got to Washington, she stopped returning my calls. Stupid stuff. What does it matter, anyway? A couple of love letters out into the void, and nothing back. I wonder if she even read them. It's embarrassing to think about, now, that I got all worked up.

Though, technically, I guess, I still get all worked up. So maybe I haven't achieved all the, uh, perspective that I'm supposed to, at least not yet. I just know that I don't feel like talking about it, or going over all the gory details for your voyeuristic pleasure. It's really none of your fucking business.

"Toby, I'd like to talk to you again about trying a trial medication."

And I'd thought we'd made it through the woods relatively unscathed. My neck and back ache from trying to sit up straight and look forthright. If this has been his plan, I wish he'd said it from the beginning.

"Doc, I don't know. I mean, no offense, but I figure that this is normal for a kid my age. I can see why you'd think that. I figure that I'm just as screwed as everyone else, I just notice it more, if that makes sense. I mean, isn't this kind of thing normal for someone who gets dumped?"

Martin purses his lips and shakes his head slightly as he speaks. He makes a little open-palm gesture with his hands, which I think is supposed to imply that he is leveling with me.

"I'd like to try a trial dosage for awhile. From what you've told me, you've had these feelings for quite a while, and that, combined with your problems sleeping, means that medication could be a good temporary measure."

I shrug.

Bird is squinting at me, already buzzed.

"He says that it's just a trial dosage. I mean, he seemed pretty insistent. At this point it would be like breaking out the kitchen knives not to go along," I tell him.

Bird shrugs and puts his hands behind his head.

"Well, if he thinks it will help."

I take another drag off my cigarette, which is now done.

"Do you think I'm getting better?"

"Sure you're getting better. I've always said, a little self-medication is all you need."

"Yeah. Maybe. Pass that over here, will ya?"

The wind is low. It's cool for a fall night. I think it may even be getting cold. This is our usual spot, though it's nicer in the summer. We parked Bird's hatchback at the end of the road. He thought it would be a good idea to come up here and relax a bit with some good old ganja. I'm not sure it's helping that much, though. I'm just getting dumb and a little paranoid.

"You should try it," Bird is saying. "I mean, what is the real logical difference between a little bit of self-medication like we've got going on here and something which is, shall we say, imposed by an external source? Or, at least, suggested?"

I shrug and try to articulate.

"No, it's not the logical difference. I mean, look. I'm just worried. It's not that I like being unhappy."

"No, that would be logically infeasible," Bird says, and seeing that I am not going to hit the water pipe, takes it back from me. He scrambles around for the lighter.

Deciding I need to clear my head, I stand and face him.

"No, it's just that – look, Bird, I mean, I've been fighting this thing so long, you know? I've begun to like, define myself by my depression. I mean, I don't even want to call it depression, that's my shrink's description. To me, it's just the way I am. I mean, aren't you worried that I'll be different? That it will be horrible somehow?"

Bird is looking at me blearily, his head leaning against a log.

"Dude, if it will help you be happier, how bad could it be?"

Suddenly I'm just tired of arguing about it. I stare at him.

"Whatever. Just give me a hit off that thing," I say.

I sit down again and take another hit.

Oh, well. How bad could it be, really? I mean, other than bitching for my own amusement, and the occasional false epiphany brought about by chronically low levels of serotonin, what I am really giving up?

That last hit has really put me over the edge, and I can barely think at all any more.

The question to ask yourself is, does the fact that it is all cliché, that it has all been done before and will be done again, better and more fully, does that make loving Jen so passionately, so violently, somehow less? Does the fact that every teenager probably falls in love with the first person they have sex with decrease the strength of my own feeling? Can I still find sanctity and validity in this thing called love? And more importantly, did she love me?

I'm beginning to feel really sad. Getting stoned like this just makes me miss Jen too much. I am aching just to talk to her. I don't know why I even do this anymore.

It has been just two months, and I really feel much better now. I don't know why I did not try this solution before. Dr. Martin and I have made a lot of progress now, and I don't think that taking Prozac and lithium has changed me at all. I am still the same old Toby Grey, just happier now.

My parents have told me they are so happy that I have finally straightened up. I'm applying to Calberton University this year, and I really think that will be a good place for me. Bird will not be applying to Calberton, which is too bad, but I am okay with that.

I also think the antidepressants I am taking are not the real reason I feel so much better. Sure, they may help, but it is a question of how one fundamentally views the world. Now I can see both the positive and negative side of things, and I think that is good. I don't miss Jen so much, and that is because I can better put that whole experience in perspective. I can now see that really I was being melodramatic about a sophomoric, juvenile experience that is ultimately not very important in my life. I also think that sex before marriage may have done me psychic harm, and I have been considering whether it is really such a good idea to experiment with that kind of emotional heaviness before I am truly ready.

I'm not sure how I feel about that, but one thing I know for certain is that I am getting better and that it makes me so happy to be able to know that much for sure.

Indian Summer

On July 11th, in the summer of 1995, a young man named Stephen Moon shot himself out on the plains outside the town of White Horse, South Dakota. He had left the reservation sometime in the afternoon on his four-wheeled scooter. When he hadn't come home seven hours later, the Pine Ridge Reservation Search and Rescue Team — which consisted of two volunteers, Bill and Ed — was dispatched. They found his body less than a mile out of Pine Ridge.

The official report stated that Stephen was riding on his scooter chasing after a rabbit when his scooter bucked, throwing him. They said his gun must have accidentally gone off, shooting him through the head. The bullet traveled up from his chin through his right eye, collapsing part of his face.

What to do about his wake was a source of major debate among the Christian Youth Outreach Program temporarily situated in White Horse. The males in the group, namely Paul, Greg, and Nick, thought that it was better to stick with their previous plan and continue traveling around South Dakota. Nick was particularly vocal.

"We have met our requirement here," he argued. "We can do better over in Leaning Tree or anywhere else the YMCA sends us." His comments received some nods from the rest of the group. Most of them were tired of setting up a day care center every day, only to have scant turnout and no budget. They wanted to feel like they were doing something to help the people on the reservation, not just sitting around watching a bunch of little kids because they couldn't think of something better to do.

Sarah decided it was time to say something.

"We came here to help in any way possible. Now I know that we weren't told to help out in this particular case. And I know that we have no obligation to do so. But helping out at a time like this is exactly the kind of thing we came here for. Isn't it?"

Lucy and Maggie both nodded. It was true. This was exactly the kind of thing they were meant to do. It took some more arguing, but finally Greg relented, followed quickly by Paul. Nick acted sullen for a bit afterward, keeping away from the rest of the group for most of the day. But eventually he came around. They would stay to help out with the wake.

Which meant they had to move out of the community center. The wake was to be held in the only space where it could fit, the broad empty hall that they'd been calling their home. They moved out onto the plains that afternoon. Since the six of them had brought only one tent, it seemed polite to give it to the girls. The guys would all sleep in the car for the next couple of nights until the wake was over.

Lillian, their local coordinator, received the news that they'd be staying with relief.

"You can help me cook for the wake," she said, and sent them out to buy food in Dupree. They bought flour, sugar, rhubarb, hamburger meat, buffalo meat, venison, bologna, chicken, watermelon, ice cream, corn, and Hi-C drink mix. When they got back, Lillian gave the women the task of cleaning and cutting up thick chunks of buffalo meat for stew. The men offered to help but were shooed out and told to start decorating.

Stephen had written down in his journal how he wanted the wake to be held; he had thought he would die in a rodeo someday and had planned for that eventuality by laying out specific instructions. He asked for the walls to be decorated with alternating orange and black streamers, spreading down from where the middle of the wall met the ceiling like "rays of sunshine." The ceiling was to be decorated with an alternating black and blue "wheel spoke" pattern emanating from the center of the room. There were few chairs in the center, and hanging the streamers turned out to be quite a chore, as for some reason the tape didn't stick well to the walls.

Stretching up and down was hurting Greg's back to no end. When they were finished, Nick commented that the place looked like some twisted Halloween party. Paul said that that wasn't funny and that Nick should have more respect.

When they assembled for a short dinner, the girls' arms were covered up to their elbows in blood, and they stank of buffalo meat. Nick opened his mouth to say something funny, but one look from Sarah made him think better of it. They ate in sullen silence before going off to their respective beds.

That night was hot out on the plains. A dry wind swept down from the north as if someone had opened a gigantic oven and the heat were pouring out. The stars were covered with clouds, and in the distance muted flashes of lightning preceded muffled thunder. Greg looked out the back window of the trunk of the Suburban. Paul was sleeping soundly in the back seat. Out the back window Greg could see a small pool of dry prairie lit by one of the few yellow street lights and beyond that only darkness. Every once in a while he saw a flash and counted off the seconds. Ten Mississippi, eleven Mississippi, twelve Mississippi. It was so flat he thought he could see clear out to Yorksville, Montana. He wondered what his family was doing there right now. Turning his back to the window, he lay on top of his sleeping bag, trying to get comfortable.

The heat was oppressive. Nick cracked the passenger seat window until he heard the mosquitoes get in, then thought better of it. He tried to protect himself by covering his head with his sleeping bag, but the heat became too much. But every time he exposed his head, just as he was about to fall off to sleep a mosquito would whine by his ear. The whining would stop abruptly, and Nick would spasm, slapping a random part of his body. He couldn't tell whether his efforts were successful. Another damn whining would happen a moment later.

They hadn't had this problem in the community center. There the floor was dry and cool, and you could breathe. They had screens, so a nice breeze could be felt without letting every damn bug in. Greg could hear Nick rustling in the front. He hoped he'd cut it out, so that maybe they both could get some shut-eye.

The next day was unending tedium. Pews had to be moved over one at a time from the church located on the other side of town. Lillian insisted it was town tradition, and nobody could think of grounds to argue.

The boys took turns carrying them over while the girls swept, mopped, and dusted the community center, getting it ready for the arrival of the corpse. Each surface had to be gone over with soapy water. All finished wood had to be wiped with Orange Glow. The sticky antiseptic smell hung over everything, till Sarah swore she was going to throw up.

The guys weren't making much headway with the pews. They were very awkward to carry. The bottoms kept cutting into Paul's shins. Each time he banged his legs, Paul would drop the off-balance mess and swear. He began walking with a limp, until he stopped trying altogether and kneeled in the dust.

"I think my shins are bleeding." He rolled up his pant leg, and indeed they were. Greg made a hollow whistling sound.

"Let me carry some for awhile. It's my turn anyway."

Greg and Nick picked up the pew and shuffled a few steps before Nick dropped the edge on the back of his calf. They could see the community center a few hundred feet away, hazy in the heat.

That night it rained, and though each boy was sunburned and sticky, they were thankful to be relatively dry. The girls' thin tent didn't have a chance. The weak nylon was quickly soaked through.

Maggie turned on a flashlight, playing it over their cramped sleeping quarters. The water had seeped down the sides into the floor, right over their ineffective ground sheet. She reached out to the walls. They were damp to the touch. Everything was going to get wet.

Lucy groaned.

"Jesus, Maggie, turn the light off."

Maggie swung the light over and pointed it at Lucy's face. She squinted and turned away.

"And don't shine that in my eyes."

"Sorry."

Maggie switched off the light.

As Sarah's eyes adjusted to the darkness, the tent walls glowed green. She wondered where the light came from at night. It seemed she'd never get to sleep. She could feel the water seeping through the sides of her sleeping bag. She tried to roll over to one side to get away from it, bumping into Lucy lying next to her, who groaned. She rolled back and landed in what felt like a small puddle. It seemed she'd just have to bear it.

The people began arriving the next day around twelve. Cars packed into the tiny parking lot next to the center till they overflowed onto the nearby fields. People came from all over the rez, some who didn't even seem to know Stephen.

"They come for the food," Lillian told Greg, and took another rack of potato rolls out of the oven. The body had arrived sometime in the morning, before anybody in the youth group was awake. Stephen's mother took up residence soon thereafter.

The service began at around three. Because Stephen's mother, Debbie Moon, was Sioux and his father was Christian, a compromise had been reached. Both Christian and Lakota ceremonies would be performed. The preacher arrived at two and took a seat out of the way. The holy man

arrived at two thirty, paid his respects to Debbie, and shuffled over to an open pew.

Old people gathered in silent groups outside the center,
smoking cigarettes. Kids played in the streets, bouncing.
They would play tag all through the night. The parents made
no attempts to stop them.

Conversations were engaged in openly, in those lyrical
Indian question-statements, not hushed up as if to avoid em-
barrassment.

Stephen was laid out against the wall. His school tro-
phies were set on a table next to the coffin, his picture set in
a frame in the middle. He'd won two first-place ribbons riding bulls in the rodeo. In addition, he'd won a small medal
for winning a school spelling bee. He had been only nineteen.

Nick stood around uncomfortably. He'd asked Lillian if
there was anything for them to do. She had shaken her head.

"Afterward we can serve the food. For now, just help old
people find their way to a seat."

But he hated doing that. They all smelled of cigarettes
and too much perfume, too much makeup. He didn't mind
being helpful. No problem helping out; he was eager to do it,
just being a good citizen and all. But he was sick of working
so hard every day. He was sick of nobody doing anything
around this reservation. Why couldn't they help them damn
selves?

He walked to the front and met Sarah.

She gave him a warning glance.

"Help her to her seat, will you?"

He forced a smile and gently took the lady's arm. Sarah
rolled her eyes and greeted the next guest.

Nick tried to coax the old lady into an open chair at the
back of the pews, but apparently she wanted to sit in the
front. He tried to be patient, but it was hard, with her tiny
half steps and wandering cane. They slowly walked down the
center aisle toward the casket.

She didn't stop at the first pew, but went up to Stephen's mother. They hugged, and the old woman said some words of sympathy. Nick stood around feeling useless. The old lady reached out her hand for support and began hobbling over to the corpse.

Stephen was laid out as if he were resting, his hands crossed over his stomach. His face had been rebuilt so that the family could have an open coffin. They'd rebuilt most of the left side. He looked like a wax figure. Tiny flies crawled over his lips. They were sewn shut. His whole face looked like someone had applied far too much stage makeup to a mannequin.

The old woman bent over and kissed Stephen's forehead, patting his hands. She said a short prayer, then raised her head. She turned to Nick.

"He was a good boy. He would have been a good man."

Then she hobbled off alone to sit by herself on the first pew.

After the preacher had said a few words at the micro-phone, the holy man got up to the podium. Instead of launching into a sermon, he began to sing.

He sang in that peculiar Indian way, a high-pitched wail with a harsh edge. Children were hushed. Parents bowed their heads. He sang on and on, a steady invisible beat thrumming through his voice. When he finished, the Lakota words died in his throat. He did not stop so much as subside. The old Lakota holy man shuffled off the stage to sit down again, and people moved on.

The body was taken away, and Maggie helped Lucy spread tablecloths out neatly. The food line began. The whole kitchen counter was filled, the trays spilling over onto small tables erected haphazardly. Lillian served venison stew while Greg handed out sloppy joes. Maggie manned the fried chicken and macaroni salad table. For dessert there was fried dough and Wo-Japi, a thick berry sauce in which to dip the dough. There were also cakes of every variety, chocolate, strawberry, and vanilla. Rhubarb and apple pies, watermelon, and fresh strong coffee.

Everybody laughed and chatted. Once the food was gone, people said their good-byes and pulled out, until the Christian Youth Group was left with the mess and the job of cleaning up.

It started innocently enough. Nick was doing his best to mop the floor when Maggie spilled a bucket by mistake, sploshing water all over him. He laughed and poked her with the mop. She giggled and chucked a sponge at his head, which hit Greg.

Soon, everybody was filling empty buckets and bowls with water, throwing soapy water around. The water began piling up on the floor until there were several inches. Everybody was soaked. Through Sarah's shirt you could see her pink bra. When Paul pointed it out with a smirk she laughed and threw a cup of water in his face, then ran to get more.

When they were done, the community center was far cleaner than it had to be. They gave it a chance to dry and left for the tent and car, to gather their stuff to move back in.

The sky was clear, and cool evening air prickled Sarah's skin. She walked with Nick out to the car to get their backpacks. He said he'd never seen so many stars.

How to Survive New England Weather

I met Sue at a T stop in the middle of Boston, at what they used to call Sculley Square Station. She's not the center of the story; it's not about her really. But she's part of it.

How did it start? Well, she looked so tired. She was a disordered sort of beautiful. In the train she was hanging by her arm like a rag doll, swinging with the movement of the car, her knuckles white. I felt bad for her; my heart went out to her, I guess. I offered her my seat. She thanked me and took it. We started talking. She lived near Boston too, and she'd grown up locally, and sure we could go for coffee. I remember feeling lucky even then. We got married in August of that year, three years ago now. She got me to quit smoking.

But that's not what this story is about, not really. I own a cabin in the middle of the woods. I think the trees around the cabin are probably worth more than the cabin itself. The refrigerator is fifty years old; it buzzes occasionally but works fine. The furniture is all wood with stuffy cushions tied on top. The bed is as old as the place itself, a giant metal job that has to be moved in pieces. The decorations are plain, and looking down from above the door is my shotgun, a bit dusty but still quite workable, I hope.

It's rustic, surely. It has electricity and water, and that's about it. No TV, no heating, no phone. Now it had been a mild December so far, so I wore only a sweater and thick wool underwear and wool socks, as well as my steel-toed leather boots. It was nice to return to a routine. I picked up groceries in town and drove on up into the woods. The cabin was dark but hospitable. The shingles looked like they needed replacing, but the cabin isn't worth it. Besides, replacing shingles is such arduous work. When I was a younger man, before I even started working at Sable and Co., I was a carpenter.

Replacing shingles is one of those things you need to sneak up on. If you say to yourself, I'm going to replace the shingles today and think through all the work it will take — buying the new shingles, waiting for good weather, pulling up the old, putting down the Tyvek, and then layering them down one row at a time — well, you'll never do it. The thought of all that pain and work paralyzes you. You've got to sneak up on a job like that. Don't think about it directly, just order the shingles and wait, like you might not actually do it, but you want to leave your options open. That's the way you have to do most hard things.

I put all the groceries away and open a beer.

By the time I finish it, I figure I should stretch my legs, so I walk down my driveway a ways until it meets up with the road. It is a tolerable half-hour walk to the general store from my house. There's nothing quite like a nice day in Maine in winter. Sunlight streams down plentifully but somehow loses the power to warm. The pine trees are the only things with any green; everything else is stark naked. In spring the fields are covered with wildflowers, dandelions padding everything in yellow. But in winter the landscape seems to be scratching the sky, and there is nothing but the dull color of dying straw.

People coming to New England for the first time in winter love to talk about just how much snow there is. They frolic gaily about, and build snowmen, and throw the stuff at each other when there's barely a dusting on the ground. It's such a refreshing change of pace for some. But then the days turn into weeks, and the snow keeps on coming. It keeps piling up until it's so thick that the whole world seems frozen, and you have to salt your front walk and driveway even though the salt sticks to everything. Your porch and house become covered with white residue from boots and mittens and the other mandatory vestments of the season. The nights become longer, until the day is a brief interlude between periods of utter blackness. Once you've stayed long enough, you won't marvel at all the pretty snow. You'll shiver and hurry about and stamp your feet when you get inside, just like a local, and thank God for central heating and indoor plumbing.

Frozen leaves crunch underneath my feet, and the air rips through my lungs. It occurs to me that I can buy a pack of cigarettes. I hadn't had a cigarette in a long time. This is the place, this is the weather for it. I've always found that cold weather is easier to bear with a cigarette or twenty.

I am happy to find the general store open, as today most everything else is closed. The man behind the counter is surprised to see me, a non-local on a holiday when it's not even hunting season. I buy two packs of Marlboros and a bottle of Jack Daniel's and a box of Dead Eye buckshot. He asks me what I am doing tomorrow, whether my shopping is done, and whether I have family around here. He's just being polite. I edge toward the door as he wishes me a Merry Christmas and push my way back out into the cold.

I light my cigarette on the stoop. My lungs offer weak resistance before the smoke forces its way down, coiling through my system, and I feel my muscles for the first time in a long time begin to relax.

I start home, carefully holding the bottle through the brown bag in one hand, and shove the packs of cigarettes into my pants pockets. I put the box of buckshot into the pocket of my coat. I am feeling pretty good at this point; the cigarette is giving me a pleasant buzz, my reward for falling from grace after such a long abstention.

For a month or so, I kept thinking she was coming back. I kept pretty calm for a while. Sure, we had fights, but generally it was swell. It was great. It was only recently I noticed she was drifting. She just seemed distracted. The worst was in bed. It was like we were foreign objects, thrown into the mix together. It was like she was over there, and I was over here, and we were having sex over the phone. Then one day she put down her fork at breakfast and calmly told me it was over. I'm okay about it now. Then it was really hard for me, but now I can see why.

Usually, though, I like to think about how it could have gone differently. In my head, I go through how it should have happened. We'd get into this big fight. And she'd throw her clothes into a suitcase, and she'd dump her CDs in on top, all disordered. But she'd leave most everything else. She would be so angry, she'd just storm out into the snow and take a cab. Sometimes she makes it to the cab before I stop her and convince her just to stay the night, because after all it's cold out there, and you're only wearing your slippers.

Sometimes she is so angry she goes through the whole apartment and takes everything that is hers, leaving nothing behind, and we get into a screaming argument about who should get the picture from Venice that we both love so much and both paid for. Those times she gets halfway to the door before I stop her and tell her I love her and that she should stay, that I'm sure we can mend the gap. My mind becomes distracted. It's hard to get away from it, which I suppose is one of the reasons I came up to Maine.

Maybe I play up the melodrama, make it out to be more than it was. Maybe I should try harder to stop thinking about it. Maybe it's not such a big deal. It's my own fault, really.

It begins to rain. The nicotine helps me ignore the weather for a while, but it is thick rain, and the paper bag with the bottle of whiskey becomes slick in my grip. The bleak landscape is lost behind shifting sheets of gray. My sweater soaks through, but my feet are warm at least, until water starts to wind its way down my socks into my boots. I trudge back up to the cabin, shivering and chain smoking, trying not to notice that I'm freezing to death.

When I get home, I change out of my clothes and take a long shower. I get dressed in some dry clothes and light another cigarette. I set one of my new packs of Marlboros on the table in my study and leave the other one in my jacket.

From my desk, I can look out into the woods. I rummage around in the cupboard until I find two glasses, which I set out on the desk next to my typewriter. I tap my ashes from my cigarette into one of the glasses, pour some whiskey into the other, and wonder what to do now. A nice layout is set before me, paper on one side, a notepad on the other, and my cigarettes and the bottle all within easy reach. I sit down and try to build up some resolution, and then decide I'm hungry.

I go down to the kitchen and make myself a ham sandwich. The rain is splattering against the window, and I decide to have another drink with my sandwich, so I pour myself some whiskey and sit back and watch the day darken. The clouds are so thick that darkness is coming on fast, and I can't tell what time it is. I decide it must be night. I sip my whiskey. Gradually, I hear a gnawing scrape as the frozen rain claws at the windows. I turn on the radio, and after a while the announcer interrupts the incessant Christmas carols to declare that a snowstorm is coming and that all residents in southern Maine should be prepared, but to have a Merry Christmas all the same.

I turn the radio off and finish off my drink. I eat the last of my sandwich, have another whiskey, and sit down in front of the typewriter. With a whiskey in one hand and a cigarette in the other, I wonder idly about flammability and liquids. I pretend I'm a successful author, some famous alcoholic, settling down to write the great American novel.

I feel like Hemingway for a moment, until I remember why I came up here. How did he do it again? The typewriter beckons to me. I sip my whiskey, and I can't think of anything worth leaving. There's no one left to read it anyway.

It happens that way sometimes. Usually it was my colleagues at Sable who invited us to Christmas dinner. But in my view they're the ones to blame in the first place. A whorehouse in Chicago, a business trip. Peter may have encouraged me with his smirking looks, nasty teeth, and winks. Maybe he convinced me after three whiskeys, but I knew Peter and where he was going. And the typewriter is still sitting in front of me, dead. I stare out the window at the trees and finish my drink and think.

Suddenly I feel very melodramatic. Like cheating on your wife isn't that big of a deal, like I'm blowing this whole thing out of proportion, and I'm just being silly.

Then I pour myself another drink and figure that I might as well get on with it. So I take my old shotgun down off the wall and take down the cleaning kit from the old cedar box next to it. I work the old rag over the outside and inside, wipe off some of the dust. I work a brush down the barrel and gently clean every inch, then lock it back; it's a double-barreled mechanism, an old bastard of a gun. I walk over to my coat and take out the box of buckshot. I open the break, load it with a double shot of buck shot, snap it back again. and place it on the table next to the typewriter.

I have another cigarette and another drink, only I figure I don't really need a glass, so I start in on the bottle directly. Right about now is when it really starts to snow.

I should tell you the truth, really. She left me because she had cancer. She left me because she was dying and was in so much pain she didn't want to add to mine.

She left because I had cancer. No, because I have AIDS. I have AIDS, which I got from the woman in Chicago, and I'm dying, and she couldn't stand to see me so sick. It hurt her too much to watch me suffer. She got lonely. Well, aren't I lonely?

She got hit by a car. It's not her fault, it's not my fault, it's not anyone's fault. These things just happen. It was drugs. A mental problem. She got a better job. I wasn't her sign. I didn't smell right. I couldn't talk to her. There was something wrong with me. There is nothing wrong with me.

Then why am I doing this?

I tap my ashes into my makeshift ashtray and miss, getting them on the fine wood table. It's funny, once Sue and I made love on this table. Then we were too in love to notice we were cold. I remember how romantic I thought *The Sun Also Rises* was; of course that was set in Spain, wasn't it? Spain is always warm.

I figure that one can only dally about these things so long. I set the shotgun on the typewriter. I am careful in this; I am drunk, so it would be easy to fire too early or screw this up. There is a good two feet between the trigger and my face, and I figure to have arms fully extended is inelegant. I have a brilliant idea of how to overcome the technical logistics: I flip the typewriter around, and lodge the line return bar next to the trigger, gently working that long metal arm through the eyelet. It is lodged rather firmly in there, a good tug should work the trigger. Sue always said I was technically inclined. I sit back, admiring my handiwork.

I take a drag from my cigarette — it is half done now — and take another swig from the bottle. When I finish my cigarette, I place the bottle carefully on the table. I lean forward until my nose is brushing the mouth of the gun. I can feel my blood settle. I open my mouth and carefully encircle the mouth of the gun. The coldness of the metal makes my teeth ache.

I take a deep breath through my nose, and I am wheezing. My eyes are tearing up now. I grasp the shaft of the gun in both hands, and brace myself to pull. Quickly, like removing a Band-Aid. My body cringes. I close my eyes.

I'm waiting for something. It should come; it will be a sign, and then I'll know. I can stand the cold a little longer. I just need a push. It will come any minute now. Any second. I wait.

Existential Dilemma

Two people, Ray and Jane, are sitting on a couch in a college dorm room. The floor is strewn with junk: newspapers, a pizza box, a bouncy ball, pens, papers, notebooks, and textbooks. Jane is reading a book and taking notes. Ray is reading a magazine. There is one door in the back wall of the room.

Ray: Hey, Jane?

Jane: *[not looking up]* Yeah.

Ray: What would you do if you were about to die?

Jane: Panic, probably.

Ray: Suppose you had a lethal form of cancer or something. What do you do?

Jane: I guess I've never really thought about it. Where do you get these morbid ideas? I think I'd spend my last days with my family.

Ray: You wouldn't do something crazy?

Jane: No.

Ray: What if you were going to die in an hour?

Jane: Like an hour from now?

Ray: Yeah.

Jane: I'd probably have one last orgasm. Why?

Ray: You never know when you're going to die. It could be at any moment. For all you know, you *could* die in an hour. These could be the last minutes of our lives.

Jane: Well then it doesn't really matter much what we do, does it?

Ray: Or maybe everything we do becomes incredibly important.

Jane: How very existential.

Ray: Come on Jane, doesn't the idea that we could die in a couple of minutes make you want to do something crazy?

Jane: No.

Ray: You don't want to break something? Or scream? Or make passionate love?

Jane: What? With you?

Ray: Yeah, with me. Let's make wild monkey sex.

Jane: Ray, I like you as a friend. I find you ugly. You understand.

Ray: What if I can prove to you that we could die at any second?

Jane: Sure, then we'd have to fuck like rabbits. Why are you going on with this?

Ray: I don't know. Sometimes I feel like nothing means anything. Have you ever thought there wasn't a God?

Jane: Ray, I have work to do. Can't we do this later?

Ray: Or that there was a god, but he wasn't like the Christian God. Not some guy on the sidelines who roots for the home team. He's active.

Jane: Or she.

Ray: We have no free will. Everything we do is orchestrated. We're just puppets.

Jane: Yeah, I think everyone wonders that sometimes.

Ray: What would you do then?

Jane: I couldn't really choose what to do, could I? Whatever I did would really be an expression of the will of someone else.

Ray: But you don't know that you have no control. What if we're all just a dream? You can't prove it isn't true.

Jane: Thank you, Descartes.

Ray: Fine. Prove me wrong.

Jane: Prove what wrong?

Ray: Prove that we're not pretend. You can't prove that we're not someone else's delusion.

Jane: Can you prove that we are? I mean, if we were characters in a movie or something, we couldn't prove it anyway, because we'd be *in the movie.*

Ray: Not a movie. There's no soundtrack. A novel.

Jane: Not a novel. We're far too boring.

Ray: A short story then. Or a play.

Jane: Fine. A play. But even characters in a play don't know they're in a play.

Ray: Why not?

Jane: Because it wouldn't be much of a play. The audience couldn't suspend *their* disbelief.

Ray: If we were in a play and I walk into the hall, I should disappear, right?

Jane: I don't know. Maybe.

Ray: Okay. Let's try it.

Ray exits into the hall.

Jane: Well?

Ray: *[from the hall]* It just looks like a hall.

Jane: Okay, now you're just being silly.

Ray reenters.

Jane: What did you expect? The hall being a hall proves that you are being ridiculous, and we should stop talking about this.

Ray: Hold on. But if we were in a play, from the audience's point of view I would have just left the stage. From our point of view nothing would change. I don't think the hall proved anything... Hey, maybe we're in a poem.

Jane: I doubt it. Nothing rhymes.

Ray: Not all poems rhyme.

Jane: What would the poem be about? An ode to my math homework?

Ray: Good point. Hey, what if we just wait till the end of the play and see what happens?

Jane: If we really are in a play, when it ends we wouldn't know it. We'd cease to exist. We'd die.

Ray: Oh, that's right. After the play is over, there's nothing. Without warning, everything vanishes — no heaven, no hell, just nothing. And not even an awareness of that.

Pause.

Okay, now I'm freaking myself out.

Jane: Only if you really believe we're in a play. And you're an atheist. Maybe all good characters go to happy character heaven.

Ray: Why not? Even if you're right, and I can't prove that we're not in a play, that doesn't mean that we aren't. Just that I can't prove that we are.

Jane: And the cycle of skepticism continues. But if we *are* in a play, it's a long damn play. I'm twenty years old, and I can account for at least thirteen of those years.

Ray: Ah, but those memories could be part of the play as well. This play could only have started a moment ago, or an hour ago. *[with dramatic emphasis]* In fact, it could be ending right now! Or now! Or ... now! *[loss of dramatic emphasis]* If I keep doing this, eventually I'll be right.

Jane: Soon, I hope.

Ray: You're right. This is boring. Let's do something else. How long do we have, anyway?

Jane: According to you, minutes. *[She stretches seductively, eyeing him to see if he reacts. He notices.]* Let's go get a Coke.

Ray: If I could just prove that we're really in a play ...

Jane: Oh, I get it! You're hoping that we *are* in a play, because then we could die at any moment, and I'd want to ... God, do you think about anything but sex?

Ray gets up and starts pacing back and forth.

Ray: No. There's got to be a way. We tried out memories, we tried the hallway ...

Jane: If this *is* a play, we're not really helping the audience suspend their disbelief.

Ray stops pacing center stage, his back to the audience.

Ray: What about the fourth wall?

Jane: The fourth wall?

Ray: The fourth wall. You know, the wall that is supposedly there for the characters but is invisible to the audience.

Jane: I know what the fourth wall is, thank you.

Ray: What if one of these walls is really not a wall?

Ray starts rummaging around on the floor.

Jane: Now how are you going to prove that?

Ray: With this.

Ray holds up a bouncy ball.

Jane: What's up with the ball?

Ray: If I bounce this ball off a wall and it doesn't come back to me, then that wall isn't really real, right?

Jane: Then I have to have sex with you, is that how this works?

Ray: That's the theory.

Jane: Wonderful.

Ray: Watch. *[He bounces it off the back wall.]*

Jane: I am so relieved.

Ray: Patience. *[bounces it off a side wall]*

Jane: Are you done yet? Let's go get a Coke.

Ray: Two more to go.

Ray throws the ball into the audience.

Both characters are frozen in place for a moment. They look at each other.

Jane: Do that again.

Ray grabs a piece of newspaper off the ground, crumples it into a ball, looks at Jane, then hesitantly throws the ball into the audience.

Ray: Well I'll be damned.

Curtain.

Afterword: An Interview with the Publisher

Interviewer: Thank you for taking time out of your busy schedule to chat with me.

Publisher: My pleasure. *[He gestures for me to get on with it.]*

I: What do you think was the main contribution to the success of *Frustrated Young Men*?

P: Clever marketing. *[He lets out a barking laugh.]*

I: No, seriously.

P: I am serious. We targeted eighteen to twenty-one-year-olds, primarily computer literate individuals in college.

I: Why such a small demographic?

P: Our primary distribution point is the Web site. We needed to reach people who use the Internet and were interested in angsty stuff like this.

I: Why did you choose to sell books through PulpLit.com?

P: I think we're entering a new age of direct interaction between artists and their audiences. We're seeing a new trend; as the cost of producing media, newspapers, books, and CDs gets cheaper, we're going to see more artists cut out the middlemen. The role of a publisher like me will be diminished to just putting up capital, making a seed investment. Really, when the threshold to putting your music on the Internet or producing your own book is so low, why not do it yourself?
I think of it as a shift from a client-server relationship for the

transmission of art to a peer-to-peer model. Instead of these giant media juggernauts like AOL and Viacom, there will be all these little publications. Instead of people sitting docilely by and passively consuming art, I see a future where people are dedicated to entertaining each other. We'll see the same democratizing power that has made the Internet a home for blogs and every media pundit transform TV into a participatory medium. You can see it already with magazines — publications like *The Kitchen Sink* [a Bay Area publication] are not aimed at achieving critical mass or becoming national. Rather, they're focused on serving the community, in providing a means for voices within the Bay Area to be read by other people in the Bay Area.

The lessons I draw from this are that if you want to succeed in this new arena, you've got to think small.

I: That's all fine, but I wanted to talk about your zine in particular, PulpLit.com.

P: The zine serves as both a call-for-submissions vehicle, so we can identify and make acquisitions, and as marketing for the books.

I: Do you feel that using other people's work as a promotional tool for the books you publish is deceptive?

P: No. No, I don't.

I: I mean, do you feel that you're misrepresenting –

P: No, we pay these people cash. And we only buy electronic rights. I mean, sometimes with poetry I think they should pay us, like the former poetry editor [Jed Krieger] suggested.

Look, selling the books is what in principle allows us to fund the zine at all. They're codependent; that's why we sell them through the site and not through Amazon.com. Also, selling over the Web site allows us to source the books from LSI [Lighting Source, Inc.], a print-on-demand distributor. This means we have very low overhead; we don't keep any stock in a warehouse. We rely on LSI to do all the logistics.

I: Isn't it also true that you feared bookstores, even Amazon, wouldn't sell the book? Or that they'd only sell it on consignment?

P: What? Who told you that? I don't have to stand for this. I only agreed to these interviews because John said that he needed to meet the minimum page count for LSI. You can't just –

I: Sir, you haven't answered the question –

P: No, you can't just sit there and tell me how to run things.

This interview is over.

John O'Brien lives and works in the San Francisco Bay Area. This is his first published book.

PulpLit Publishing is interested in new, quality fiction to be printed in limited quantities and sold over the Internet. PulpLit Publishing also produces a quarterly magazine. More information can be found online at www.PulpLit.com.

In case anyone was confused, John O'Brien was the author, editor, publisher, and interviewer in the preceding dialogues.